Nanny of the Maroons
The Warrior Queen of Jamaica

Chapter 1

The Whisper of the Hills

The dawn was still a distant promise when the hills of Jamaica stirred with an uncanny quiet. The dense greenery clung to the mist, shrouding the landscape in a cloak of secrecy. Only the rhythmic chirping of crickets and the occasional rustle of leaves disrupted the stillness. These hills, fierce and untamed, were a sanctuary—a fortress for the Maroons and their leader, Nanny.

Nanny stood at the edge of a precipice, her silhouette outlined against the pale light of the crescent moon. Her gaze was sharp, scanning the horizon where the dense foliage met the star-studded sky. She was a petite woman, but her presence was commanding. Her head was wrapped in a vibrant scarf, its edges fluttering gently in the breeze, and her spear, a polished wooden staff tipped with gleaming iron, was gripped firmly in her hand.

The land beneath her feet held stories of rebellion and resilience. For generations, the Maroons had made these hills their home, carving out lives of freedom away from the oppressive chains of colonial rule. Under Nanny's leadership, they had turned their sanctuary into a fortress, using the hills' labyrinthine paths and natural barriers to outwit their enemies. But tonight, the air was heavy with foreboding. Nanny could feel it in her bones, as though the hills themselves were whispering warnings.

"Nanny," a deep voice called from behind her.

She turned to see Kojo, her trusted lieutenant. Tall and broad-shouldered, with a scar running across his cheek, Kojo was as formidable as the land they defended. His dark eyes reflected concern as he approached, bowing his head slightly in respect.

"The scouts have returned," he said, his voice low but urgent. "The Redcoats are moving. A large force. They're coming for us."

Nanny's jaw tightened, but her expression remained calm. "How far?" she asked.

"Two days, maybe less," Kojo replied. "They're marching through the valley, heavily armed. This is no ordinary patrol. They mean to wipe us out."

Nanny's eyes narrowed, her mind already racing through possibilities. The British had grown increasingly desperate to crush the Maroons, viewing their defiance as a blight on colonial authority. But Nanny knew these hills better than anyone. She knew their secrets, their strengths, their shadows. And she knew how to turn them into weapons.

"Summon the council," she said finally. "We'll meet at first light."

Kojo nodded and disappeared into the shadows, leaving Nanny alone once more. She took a deep breath, closing her eyes and listening to the sounds of the forest. Her connection to the land was almost supernatural; some whispered that she had the gift of obeah, the spiritual power of her ancestors. Whether it was true or not, Nanny's ability to foresee danger and strategize had kept her people alive through countless battles.

As the night deepened, Nanny made her way back to the village. Hidden among the hills, the settlement was a network of thatched huts and communal spaces, illuminated by the flickering light of torches. The Maroons were a community bound by purpose and survival, each member contributing to their shared resistance. Even now, as most of the village slept, a few sentries kept watch, their eyes scanning the darkness for any sign of movement.

Nanny entered her hut, a modest structure adorned with symbols of her Ashanti heritage. A small fire crackled in the corner, casting dancing shadows on the walls. She sat cross-legged on a woven mat and unrolled a map of the surrounding terrain. Her fingers traced the valleys and ridges, the rivers and caves, as she plotted their defense. She would not allow the Redcoats to destroy what her people had built.

By the time the first light of dawn crept over the hills, the council had gathered in the village square. Men and women of all ages sat in a circle, their faces solemn. Nanny stood at the center, her voice steady as she addressed them.

"The British are coming," she announced. "Their numbers are great, but so is our strength. The hills are our allies, and together, we will make them regret stepping into our domain."

Murmurs of agreement rippled through the crowd, though the tension was palpable. Nanny raised a hand, silencing them.

"This will not be an easy fight," she continued. "But remember who we are. We are the descendants of warriors, survivors of the Middle Passage. We have tasted freedom, and we will not surrender it. Not now, not ever."

Her words ignited a spark in her people. One by one, they pledged their resolve, their voices rising in a chorus of defiance. Nanny's heart swelled with pride, but she knew the battle ahead would test them all.

As the council dispersed to prepare, Nanny lingered, her eyes scanning the hills. The whisper of the land was louder now, a symphony of warnings and promises. She gripped her spear tightly, her resolve as unyielding as the mountains around her.

"Let them come," she whispered to the wind. "We will be ready."

The preparations began in earnest. Scouts combed the dense undergrowth, setting traps along the likely paths of approach. Hunters crafted arrows dipped in poison from native plants. Women and elders prepared provisions, their hands moving swiftly as they braided food into carryable bundles and tied herbs for medicine. The air buzzed with determination, each member of the community knowing their role in the fight to come.

Nanny moved among them, offering guidance, strength, and calm. When a young boy fumbled with his bowstring, she knelt beside him, her hands steadying his trembling fingers. "Focus," she said softly. "Your heart is strong. Trust it."

The boy nodded, his fear melting under her steady gaze. Across the camp, similar scenes unfolded as Nanny's spirit infused her people with confidence. Though outnumbered and outgunned, they had an edge the British could never understand: unity, a connection to their land, and the unyielding desire for freedom.

As the sun climbed higher, an abeng sounded from the edge of the village. A scout returned, breathless and wide-eyed. "They've reached the outer perimeter," he reported. "They're moving faster than expected."

Nanny nodded. "Then so will we," she said. "Everyone to their positions."

The Maroons moved with precision, slipping into the shadows of the forest. Nanny took her place at a vantage point, her spear in hand, her eyes fixed on the path below. The land held its breath, waiting for the clash that would decide their fate.

And then, the first Redcoat appeared, his bright uniform a stark contrast to the muted greens and browns of the forest. He stepped cautiously, his musket at the ready. Behind him, more soldiers followed, their boots crunching on the forest floor.

Nanny raised her spear, the signal her people had been waiting for. From the shadows, a barrage of arrows rained down, swift and deadly. The soldiers scrambled for cover, but the forest offered them no sanctuary. The Maroons moved like ghosts, striking and disappearing before the Redcoats could retaliate.

The battle had begun, and the hills sang with the cries of defiance. Nanny's heart pounded as she led her people into the fray, her voice rising above the chaos.

"For freedom!" she shouted, her spear cutting through the air. The hills echoed her cry, a fierce anthem of resistance that would not be silenced. The fight for survival, for freedom, and for the legacy of the Maroons had begun.

Chapter 2

Shadows of the Forest

The air was thick with tension as the echoes of battle faded into the depths of the forest. The initial skirmish had gone in the Maroons' favor, but Nanny knew better than to celebrate too soon. The Redcoats were cunning, and their vengeance would be swift and unrelenting. She stood among her warriors, her gaze scanning the trees as if they could speak to her, reveal the movements of the enemy.

"We've bought ourselves time," Kojo said, his voice calm but tinged with urgency. He crouched beside a fallen soldier, retrieving a pouch of ammunition. "But not much."

Nanny nodded. Her people moved silently around her, collecting weapons and supplies left behind by the British. The Maroons had no room for waste; every musket, every knife, every scrap of fabric would be repurposed. They worked quickly, their movements fluid and rehearsed, like the forest itself was aiding them.

"Kojo," Nanny said, her tone commanding but quiet. "Send a group to reinforce the traps near the river. If the Redcoats are smart, they'll try to flank us there."

Kojo stood and nodded. "It will be done."

As he disappeared into the shadows, Nanny turned her attention to the rest of her warriors. Some were injured, their wounds hastily bandaged with strips of cloth. Others sat in small groups, whispering strategies or offering each other quiet words of encouragement. Among them was a young girl named Ama, her face streaked with dirt but her eyes bright with determination. She held a small knife, its blade glinting in the dappled sunlight.

"Ama," Nanny called, beckoning her forward. "What have you learned today?"

The girl straightened her back, clutching the knife tightly. "To move like the wind, silent and unseen," she said, her voice steady.

Nanny's lips curved into a faint smile. "Good. And remember, the forest is your ally. It hides you, protects you, and fights with you. Never forget that."

Ama nodded solemnly and returned to her group. Nanny watched her for a moment, pride swelling in her chest. The future of the Maroons rested on the shoulders of the young, and it was her duty to prepare them for the battles ahead.

A rustling in the underbrush drew Nanny's attention. She tightened her grip on her spear, her eyes narrowing. From the shadows emerged a figure, his hands raised in a gesture of peace. It was Kwame, one of the scouts Nanny had sent to track the enemy's movements. His face was drawn, his breathing labored.

"Nanny," he gasped. "The Redcoats are regrouping. They've called for reinforcements, and they're setting up a camp near the river."

Nanny's jaw tightened. The river was a vital lifeline for her people, its waters providing sustenance and a natural barrier against invasion. If the British gained control of it, the Maroons' position would be compromised.

"How many?" she asked.

Kwame shook his head. "Too many to count. But they're weary, and their supplies are limited. They'll need time to fortify their camp."

Nanny turned to her warriors, her voice rising above the murmurs. "We cannot let them take the river. Tonight, we strike. Kwame, guide us to their camp. Kojo, gather the strongest among us. We'll use the cover of darkness to our advantage."

Her warriors nodded, their expressions resolute. They trusted Nanny's instincts, her ability to lead them through even the most dire of circumstances. The sun dipped lower in the sky, casting long shadows across the forest floor. Nanny took a deep breath, feeling the weight of her responsibility but also the strength of her resolve.

As night fell, the Maroons moved like phantoms through the forest. The abeng sounded again, its haunting call echoing through the trees and signaling the start of their assault. Nanny led the charge, her spear glinting in the moonlight as she moved with practiced precision. The Redcoats' camp came into view, their fires flickering weakly against the encroaching darkness.

The Maroons struck swiftly and without warning. Arrows rained down from the trees, followed by a barrage of spears and stones. The British soldiers scrambled to defend themselves, but the Maroons' attack was relentless. Nanny fought at the forefront, her movements a blur of speed and strength. She was everywhere at once, her voice rallying her warriors and striking fear into the hearts of their enemies.

The battle raged on, the forest alive with the sounds of conflict. But as the first light of dawn broke through the canopy, it became clear that the Maroons had won. The Redcoats' camp lay in ruins, their forces scattered. Nanny stood at the edge of the battlefield, her spear planted firmly in the ground. Her people gathered around her, their faces a mixture of exhaustion and triumph.

"This is our land," she said, her voice carrying the weight of their shared victory. "And we will defend it with everything we have. Let this be a lesson to those who dare to challenge us."

The Maroons raised their voices in a triumphant cheer, their spirits renewed. Though the battle was won, Nanny knew the war was far from over. But as she looked out over her people, she felt a surge of hope. They were strong, united, and unyielding. Together, they would endure.

The forest, once again, fell silent, its shadows embracing the victorious Maroons. The fight for freedom continued, but for now, the hills stood as a testament to their resilience and defiance. And at their heart was Nanny, the warrior who had turned the land itself into a weapon of liberation.

Chapter 3
The Gathering Storm

The victory at the river had brought the Maroons a momentary reprieve, but Nanny's heart was far from settled. She stood on the ridge overlooking the camp, her spear resting beside her, as the warm hues of dusk painted the horizon. Below her, the Maroons moved with quiet determination, repairing weapons, tending to the wounded, and fortifying their defenses. Despite their triumph, the threat of the Redcoats loomed larger than ever.

Kojo approached her, his face shadowed with worry. "Nanny, the scouts have returned with troubling news. The Redcoats are amassing an even larger force. They've brought reinforcements from the coast."

Nanny's lips pressed into a thin line. "How many?"

Kojo hesitated. "Hundreds, maybe more. They're determined to crush us."

Nanny's gaze turned back to the horizon. "Then we must prepare," she said firmly. "Gather the council. Tonight, we plan."

As darkness fell, the council convened in the heart of the village. The abeng sounded, summoning leaders and warriors to the meeting circle. The firelight flickered across their faces, reflecting both fear and resolve.

Nanny stood in the center, her presence commanding as she addressed them.

"The British think they can overwhelm us with their numbers," she began, her voice steady and strong. "But they do not understand what it means to fight for freedom. They fight for power and greed. We fight for our lives, our families, and our future. And that makes us stronger than they can ever be."

The warriors nodded, their expressions hardening with determination. Kojo stepped forward, spreading a map of the surrounding terrain on the ground.

"We know their supply lines run through the lowlands," he explained. "If we disrupt their supplies, we weaken them. They'll have to retreat."

"And the reinforcements?" asked Kwame, his voice low but firm.

"We lure them into the hills," Nanny interjected. "The forest is our ally. We'll divide their forces and strike where they're weakest. They won't know where we're coming from until it's too late."

A murmur of approval rippled through the council. Nanny's strategies had never failed them, and her ability to outthink the British had become legendary among her people. Yet, the weight of the task ahead was evident in their eyes.

"This will not be easy," Nanny continued, her gaze sweeping over the gathered faces. "We'll need every man, woman, and child ready to defend our home. Everyone has a role to play. And remember, our greatest weapon is not our spears or arrows, but our unity. Together, we are unstoppable."

The council dispersed, each leader returning to their groups to relay the plans. Nanny lingered by the fire, her mind racing. She knew the next battle would be unlike any they had faced before. The British were growing desperate, and desperation made them dangerous.

As the village settled into a restless quiet, Nanny walked to the edge of the camp. The stars above glittered like scattered diamonds, their light softening the harsh edges of the night. She closed her eyes, reaching out to the spirits of her ancestors.

"Guide us," she whispered. "Give us the strength to endure. Let our courage honor those who came before us."

The wind stirred the leaves, carrying with it a sense of calm. Nanny took a deep breath, the weight on her shoulders feeling slightly lighter. She turned back to the camp, her resolve renewed.

In the days that followed, the Maroons moved with a sense of purpose. Scouts scoured the land, mapping enemy movements and identifying weaknesses. Traps were laid along the likely paths of the British advance, and caches of supplies were hidden in the forest. Even the children played their part, acting as messengers and lookouts.

Nanny trained tirelessly with her warriors, honing their skills and preparing them for the fight to come. She sparred with Kojo, their wooden staffs clashing with sharp cracks in the humid air. Despite her small stature, Nanny was a formidable opponent, her speed and precision unmatched.

"You've taught us well," Kojo said, breathing heavily as he lowered his staff. "But will it be enough?"

Nanny met his gaze, her expression unwavering. "It will have to be."

As the sun dipped low on the eve of battle, the Maroons gathered once more. Nanny stood before them, her spear in hand, her voice rising above the murmurs of the crowd.

"Tomorrow, we face a great challenge," she said. "But remember this: we are not just fighting for ourselves. We fight for every soul that dreams of freedom. We fight for those who came before us and those who will come after. And we will win, because we are Maroons. We are free, and we will never be broken."

A roar of defiance erupted from the crowd, their voices echoing through the hills. As the night deepened, Nanny stood at the edge of the camp, watching as her people prepared for the battle to come. The storm was gathering, but she was ready to face it.

The hills, silent witnesses to centuries of struggle, seemed to hum with anticipation. Nanny gripped her spear tightly, her heart steady. The fight for freedom was far from over, but she knew one truth above all: the Maroons would never yield.

Chapter 4
The Clash of Forces

The dawn arrived cloaked in gray, the sun hidden behind thick clouds that seemed to mirror the weight in Nanny's heart. She stood at the edge of the Maroon camp, overlooking the valley below where the Redcoats were beginning their advance. From her vantage point, she could see the glint of bayonets and hear the distant thud of drums marking their march.

Kojo approached her, his expression grim. "They've split their forces, as you predicted. A smaller group is moving along the eastern ridge, likely to flank us."

Nanny nodded. "Good. Let them believe they have the upper hand. Kwame's unit is already in position there. They'll make sure the Redcoats regret stepping into our territory."

Kojo's lips twitched into a faint smile. "And the main force?"

Nanny's gaze shifted to the dense forest that lined the valley. "We'll draw them in deeper. The traps are set, and the terrain will do the rest. Patience is our weapon today."

As Kojo left to relay her orders, Nanny turned her attention back to her warriors. They moved with quiet determination, their faces painted with mud and ash to blend into the forest. Every Maroon knew their role, from the youngest messenger to the eldest healer. They were not just fighting a battle; they were defending a way of life.

The abeng sounded, its haunting call echoing through the hills. It was the signal to move. Nanny gripped her spear tightly and led her warriors into the shadows of the forest. The ground beneath her feet felt alive, as though the land itself was preparing for the fight.

The first clash came suddenly. A Redcoat scouting party stumbled into one of the traps, a concealed pit lined with sharpened stakes. Their cries of alarm were cut short, silenced by the swift and deadly precision of Maroon archers. The forest seemed to swallow the sound, leaving only an eerie stillness in its wake.

Nanny's warriors moved like phantoms, striking and vanishing before the British could organize a response. The Redcoats' brightly colored uniforms made them easy targets among the greens and browns of the jungle. Arrows and spears rained down from above, while concealed warriors launched surprise attacks from the underbrush.

Nanny fought alongside her people, her movements a blur of speed and precision. She used the terrain to her advantage, striking from elevated positions and retreating into the dense foliage before the enemy could react. Her spear found its mark again and again, each thrust a reminder to the Redcoats that the Maroons would not be subdued.

The British, however, were not without their own tactics. Cannon fire tore through the trees, scattering splinters and sending warriors diving for cover. Smoke filled the air as musket volleys erupted, their deafening roars contrasting with the natural sounds of the forest. Despite their disarray, the Redcoats pressed forward, their sheer numbers threatening to overwhelm the Maroon defenders.

By midday, the battle had spread across the valley. Nanny regrouped with Kojo and Kwame near a concealed outpost. Sweat dripped from their brows, but their eyes burned with determination.

"Their main force is faltering," Kwame reported, his voice edged with urgency. "But the cannons are a problem. They've cleared a path through the northern ridge."

Nanny's mind raced. The cannons were a threat they couldn't ignore, but a direct assault would cost too many lives. She glanced at Kojo, then at the map spread before them.

"We'll split their attention," she decided. "Kwame, take your unit and harass the cannon crews. Target their supply lines and force them to reposition. Kojo, you and I will lead a strike on their command center. If we take out their officers, the rest will crumble."

The two men nodded, their trust in Nanny absolute. As they moved to carry out her orders, Nanny took a moment to center herself. She closed her eyes, feeling the pulse of the forest around her. The land was their ally, and she would wield it like a weapon.

The final hours of the battle were a blur of chaos and determination. Kwame's unit succeeded in disrupting the cannons, their hit-and-run tactics forcing the British artillery crews into disarray. Meanwhile, Nanny and Kojo's strike team infiltrated the heart of the enemy camp. Under cover of darkness, they moved with deadly precision, cutting down officers and sowing confusion among the ranks.

By the time dawn broke, the British forces were in full retreat. The valley was littered with abandoned weapons and supplies, a testament to the Maroons' victory. Nanny stood at the edge of the battlefield, her spear planted firmly in the ground. Around her, the Maroons gathered, their faces a mixture of exhaustion and triumph.

"This is our land," Nanny declared, her voice carrying over the hills. "And no force on this earth will take it from us. Let this victory be a warning to those who would challenge our freedom."

The warriors erupted in cheers, their voices echoing through the forest. Nanny's heart swelled with pride, but she knew the fight was far from over. The British would return, stronger and more determined. But so would the Maroons. They had the land, the unity, and the unyielding spirit of a people who refused to be broken.

As the sun rose higher, casting its golden light over the hills, Nanny turned her gaze to the horizon. The struggle for freedom would continue, but for now, they had won another day. And as long as she stood, spear in hand, the Maroons would endure.

Chapter 5

The Price of Victory

The battlefield was eerily quiet as the sun climbed higher, casting its golden rays over the Maroon camp. The scent of smoke lingered in the air, mingling with the earthy aroma of the forest. Nanny walked among her people, her spear in hand, her gaze scanning the aftermath of the battle. Victory was theirs, but it had not come without cost.

The wounded lay in makeshift shelters, their groans of pain a somber reminder of the price they had paid. Healers moved swiftly, applying poultices and stitching wounds with practiced precision. Children carried water and clean rags, their faces etched with a seriousness that belied their age. The village, though bruised, was alive with resilience.

Kojo approached Nanny, his arm wrapped in a bloodied bandage. Despite his injury, he stood tall, his eyes meeting hers with a mixture of pride and concern.

"The British are gone, for now," he said. "Their forces are scattered. But they'll return, and next time, they'll bring even more."

Nanny nodded, her expression unreadable. "We've bought ourselves time, but Kojo, we must do more than survive. We must prepare for the battles ahead. The British will not stop until they believe us broken."

Kojo's jaw tightened. "Then we'll make sure they never find us broken."

Nanny placed a hand on his shoulder. "Rest for now. You've done well. We've all done well."

That evening, as the village gathered around a roaring fire, the mood was both celebratory and somber. The elders told stories of past victories, their voices weaving tales of resilience and hope. Nanny listened, her mind half-focused on their words and half on the challenges that lay ahead. She knew the British's next move would be more calculated, more ruthless.

As the flames crackled, Kwame stood to address the crowd. "Tonight, we celebrate not just our victory, but our spirit," he said, his voice strong. "We have shown the British that these hills are ours. That we are a people who will not be enslaved or subdued. Let this fire remind us of the fire within our hearts."

Cheers erupted, and for a moment, the weight on Nanny's shoulders felt lighter. But as the crowd began to disperse, she rose, her presence commanding immediate attention.

"Kwame is right," she began. "We have shown our strength. But the fight is far from over. Every victory comes with a lesson, and we must learn from this one. The British will return, and when they do, we must be ready to meet them with greater strength, greater unity, and greater cunning."

The warriors nodded, their resolve mirrored in their leader's voice. Nanny's words were not just a call to arms but a reminder of their shared purpose. They were fighting for more than themselves. They were fighting for freedom, for the generations yet to come.

Over the following days, the Maroons worked tirelessly to rebuild and fortify their village. Traps were reset, new paths were carved through the forest, and stockpiles of food and weapons were replenished. Nanny led the efforts, her energy seemingly boundless. She moved among her people, offering guidance and encouragement, her presence a source of strength.

One morning, as she walked along the edge of the camp, a young boy approached her. He carried a bundle of flowers, their vibrant colors a stark contrast to the somber mood of the past days.

"For you, Nanny," he said, his voice shy but sincere. "Thank you for keeping us safe."

Nanny knelt, accepting the flowers with a soft smile. "Thank you, child. But remember, it is not just me. It is all of us. Together, we keep each other safe."

The boy nodded, his eyes shining with admiration, and ran off to join his friends. Nanny watched him go, her heart swelling with a mix of pride and determination. The children were the reason she fought so fiercely. They were the future she was determined to protect.

That night, as the village settled into an uneasy peace, Nanny stood at the edge of the ridge, gazing out over the darkened hills. The stars above shone brightly, their light unyielding even in the face of darkness. She thought of her ancestors, of the strength and wisdom they had passed down through generations. She thought of the battles yet to come and the freedom that awaited on the other side.

"We will endure," she whispered to the night. "And one day, we will be free."

The wind carried her words into the forest, where the trees seemed to echo her resolve. Nanny gripped her spear tightly, her heart steady. The fight was far from over, but she knew, with unshakable certainty, that the Maroons would prevail. Together, they would turn every challenge into another chapter in their story of resistance and triumph.

Chapter 6

Whispers of Betrayal

The morning mist clung to the forest, veiling the Maroon village in a shroud of stillness. The quiet, however, was deceptive. Nanny's instincts hummed with unease. She moved through the camp, her eyes scanning for signs of trouble, her spear a reassuring weight in her hand.

Kojo met her at the edge of the clearing, his expression tight. "The scouts returned an hour ago," he said, his voice low. "They've spotted movement on the southern ridge. Redcoats, but not many. It's strange."

Nanny's eyes narrowed. "Strange, indeed. They wouldn't send such a small group unless they were testing us. Or unless they have help."

Kojo's brow furrowed. "Help? You think someone—"

Nanny held up a hand, silencing him. Her gaze swept over the trees, as though the forest itself could confirm her suspicions. "We've faced betrayal before," she said softly. "It would not be the first time they tried to divide us from within."

Kojo's jaw tightened. "Do you think it's one of our own?"

Nanny didn't answer immediately. Instead, she turned her gaze back to the camp, where her people moved with quiet efficiency. "Trust is a fragile thing, Kojo. We must tread carefully. Call the council. We need to discuss this before taking action."

The council convened in the shaded grove near the village's heart. Leaders and warriors gathered in a tight circle, their expressions a mix of concern and determination. Nanny stood in the center, her spear planted firmly in the ground beside her.

"The Redcoats are moving again," she began, her voice steady but grave. "A small force on the southern ridge. It could be a feint, but it could also be more than that. We must consider the possibility of betrayal within our ranks."

Her words sent a ripple of unease through the group. Kwame, always quick to speak, leaned forward. "You think one of us would turn against our own? Who could do such a thing?"

Nanny met his gaze. "Fear can twist even the strongest hearts. The British are desperate, and desperation makes them dangerous. They may have promised someone safety, freedom, or something else entirely. We cannot dismiss the possibility."

"But how do we find them?" asked Ama, her voice steady despite the tension in her features. "If someone among us is feeding information to the British, they'll be careful."

"We watch," Nanny said firmly. "We listen. And we act only when we are certain. The last thing we need is to sow distrust among ourselves without cause."

The council nodded, though the air remained heavy with unease. Nanny dismissed them, her mind already racing with plans.

That night, Nanny moved silently through the camp, her senses heightened. The forest's usual symphony of sounds seemed muted, as though the land itself held its breath. She approached the edge of the village, where a narrow path wound its way toward the southern ridge. It was here that she paused, crouching low and listening.

A faint rustling caught her attention. Her grip on her spear tightened as she melted into the shadows, her eyes trained on the path. Moments later, a figure emerged, moving quickly and quietly. It was too dark to make out their face, but their movements were deliberate, purposeful. They carried a bundle, its shape indistinct in the dim light.

Nanny followed, her steps as silent as the wind. The figure moved deeper into the forest, away from the village and toward the ridge. Nanny's heart pounded in her chest, her mind racing with questions. Who was this? And what were they carrying?

Finally, the figure stopped in a small clearing. They crouched, placing the bundle on the ground and opening it. Nanny moved closer, her breath caught in her throat as she recognized the contents: a map of the village and its defenses, marked with notes in an unfamiliar hand.

Before she could act, the figure stiffened, as though sensing her presence. They turned sharply, their eyes meeting Nanny's. It was Kwame.

"Nanny," he said, his voice trembling. "I can explain."

Nanny stepped forward, her spear leveled at him. "Explain quickly, Kwame. Betrayal leaves no room for hesitation."

Kwame's shoulders sagged, his eyes filled with desperation. "They threatened my family. My sister's children. They have them, Nanny. If I didn't give them what they wanted, they'd…" He trailed off, his voice breaking.

Nanny's grip on her spear didn't waver. "And what did they promise you, Kwame? That your betrayal would save them? Do you think the British would honor their word?"

Tears streamed down Kwame's face. "I didn't know what else to do. I… I thought if I gave them just enough, they'd let them go."

Nanny's heart ached, but her resolve remained firm. "You've endangered us all. But there may still be a way to undo the damage you've done. Come with me. We'll face the council together."

Kwame hesitated, then nodded, his expression one of shame and resignation. Nanny lowered her spear but kept a close watch on him as they made their way back to the village. The fight for freedom was fraught with challenges, and betrayal was among the most painful. But Nanny knew that even in the face of such trials, the Maroons' unity must endure.

As they stepped into the camp, the first light of dawn painted the sky in hues of gold and crimson. The battle ahead would be more than one of weapons and strategy. It would be a test of trust, resilience, and the strength of their shared purpose.

Chapter 7

Trials of Trust

The village was already awake by the time Nanny and Kwame returned, the dawn's golden light casting long shadows across the clearing. Word of a secret meeting spread quickly, and by the time the council was summoned, the entire village had gathered at the edge of the grove, their faces filled with curiosity and unease.

Kwame stood in the center of the council circle, his shoulders slumped and his eyes fixed on the ground. Nanny stood beside him, her spear planted firmly in the earth. She looked out at the council, her expression somber.

"Last night, I discovered something troubling," she began, her voice steady but heavy with emotion. "Kwame has betrayed us."

A wave of gasps rippled through the crowd. Kwame flinched but said nothing, his silence a confirmation of his guilt. Nanny raised a hand to quiet the murmurs.

"Before we judge him, we must understand the circumstances," she said. "Kwame, tell them what you told me."

Kwame hesitated, then took a deep breath. His voice was shaky but clear. "The British have my sister's children. They threatened to kill them if I didn't give them information about our defenses. I thought… I thought if I gave them just enough, they would release them."

The crowd's murmurs grew louder, anger and sympathy mingling in their voices. One of the elders, a woman named Adisa, stepped forward, her piercing gaze fixed on Kwame.

"You risked all our lives," she said, her voice sharp. "What guarantee did you have that they would keep their word?"

Kwame shook his head. "None. I see that now. But I was desperate. I didn't know what else to do."

Adisa's expression softened slightly, but her voice remained firm. "Desperation is no excuse for endangering your people."

Nanny stepped forward, her voice cutting through the tension. "Kwame has made a grave mistake. But his actions were driven by fear, not malice. We must decide how to address this betrayal while preserving the unity of our community. Divided, we fall. United, we endure."

The council deliberated, their voices low and serious. After a time, Kojo rose, his face set with determination.

"Kwame's actions cannot go unpunished," he said. "But exile would weaken us further. Instead, let him prove his loyalty. He will lead a mission to rescue his family and dismantle the British's plans. Success will redeem him. Failure…" Kojo's voice trailed off, the implication clear.

The council nodded in agreement, their expressions grim but resolute. Nanny turned to Kwame, her gaze steady.

"Do you accept this trial?" she asked.

Kwame looked up, tears glistening in his eyes. "I do," he said. "I will do whatever it takes to make this right."

As preparations for the mission began, Nanny worked closely with Kwame and a small group of trusted warriors. The plan was risky, relying on stealth and speed to infiltrate the British camp and free the hostages. Every detail was scrutinized, every contingency considered.

"You must move like shadows," Nanny told them as they gathered at the edge of the forest. "The British are strong, but they are blind to the forest's secrets. Use the land to your advantage."

Kwame nodded, his expression a mix of determination and fear. He carried no weapon, only a small pouch of herbs prepared by the village healers.

"These will help if anyone is injured," he said, his voice quiet. "It's the least I can do."

Nanny placed a hand on his shoulder. "You carry more than herbs, Kwame. You carry the hope of this village. Do not let it falter."

The night was moonless, the forest shrouded in darkness as Kwame and his team approached the British camp. The Redcoats' fires glowed faintly through the trees, their smoke curling upward like ghostly tendrils. Kwame's heart pounded in his chest, but he forced himself to focus. Each step brought him closer to his family—and to redemption.

The first guard fell silently, an arrow finding its mark before he could cry out. The Maroons moved swiftly, their steps as quiet as the wind. Kwame led them to the edge of the camp, where a crude wooden cage held the hostages. His breath caught as he spotted his sister's children, their faces pale and frightened.

"Stay here," he whispered to the others. "I'll get them out."

He crept forward, his hands shaking as he worked to undo the cage's crude lock. The children's eyes widened as they recognized him, but he pressed a finger to his lips, urging them to stay quiet. Finally, the lock gave way, and he pulled the door open.

"Come," he whispered. "Quickly."

The children climbed out, their movements silent but hurried. Kwame turned to lead them back to the others, but a shout rang out, shattering the silence. A Redcoat had spotted them.

"Go!" Kwame hissed, pushing the children toward the forest. He turned to face the soldier, his hands empty but his resolve unshaken.

The Redcoat raised his musket, but before he could fire, an arrow whistled through the air, striking him in the chest. Kwame's team emerged from the shadows, their weapons at the ready.

"Move!" one of them barked, pulling Kwame toward the trees.

The escape was chaotic, the forest coming alive with the sounds of pursuit. But the Maroons knew the land far better than their enemies. They disappeared into the shadows, leaving the Redcoats confused and disoriented.

By the time they reached the village, the first light of dawn was breaking. Kwame collapsed to his knees, the children clinging to him as tears streamed down his face.

Nanny stepped forward, her expression unreadable. "You have done well," she said quietly. "But your redemption is a journey, Kwame, not a destination. Remember that."

He nodded, his voice choked with emotion. "Thank you, Nanny. For giving me a chance to make things right."

As the village celebrated the safe return of the hostages, Nanny stood apart, her gaze fixed on the horizon. The challenges they faced were far from over, but for now, the Maroons had won another battle—not just against the British, but against the forces that threatened to divide them.

Together, they would endure. Together, they would prevail.

Chapter 8
The Shadow of Retribution

The victory of Kwame's mission brought a rare moment of celebration to the Maroon village. Yet, for Nanny, the relief was fleeting. She knew the British would not take this humiliation lightly. As the forest buzzed with life and the children played with newfound joy, Nanny's mind turned to the inevitable retribution that loomed on the horizon.

By midday, Kojo returned from a scouting mission, his face grim. Nanny met him at the edge of the camp, her spear in hand.

"They're regrouping," Kojo said, his voice low. "This time, it's different. They've brought engineers and heavier artillery. They're building roads through the forest."

Nanny's brow furrowed. "They mean to cut through our defenses. They're trying to destroy the forest's advantage."

Kojo nodded. "If they succeed, it will be harder to stop them. They'll carve a path straight to our village."

Nanny turned to look at the trees surrounding them. The forest had always been their greatest ally, its dense foliage and winding paths a natural barrier against the British's advances. If the Redcoats learned to navigate it, the Maroons' sanctuary would no longer be secure.

"We won't let them succeed," she said firmly. "Call the council. We need to act before they gain a foothold."

The council convened under the shade of a massive silk cotton tree, its roots sprawling like the veins of the land. Nanny stood at the center, her presence commanding.

"The British are changing their tactics," she began, addressing the gathered leaders and warriors. "They're bringing in engineers to build roads and clear the forest. This is not just an attack on us but on the land itself. If we allow them to continue, they will strip us of our greatest defense."

Kwame, still weary but resolute, stepped forward. "What do we do? We can't face their artillery head-on."

"We don't have to," Nanny replied. "The forest is alive, and it fights with us. We will use its secrets to turn their strength into weakness. We will sabotage their efforts, strike at their supply lines, and make the forest itself an enemy they cannot overcome."

The warriors murmured their agreement, their confidence in Nanny unwavering. Kojo spread a map of the region across the ground, marking the British's progress.

"Their main camp is here," he said, pointing to a clearing near the river. "The engineers are stationed there, protected by soldiers. If we can disrupt their operations, we'll slow them down."

"And if we destroy their equipment," Ama added, "they'll be forced to retreat."

Nanny nodded. "Then that's our goal. We'll divide into small groups to strike from multiple directions. Kojo, you'll lead one team. Ama, take another. I'll lead the third."

The council dispersed to prepare, their movements purposeful and swift. The Maroons had always thrived on their ability to adapt, and this time would be no different.

Night fell, and the forest came alive with its nocturnal symphony. The Maroon warriors moved through the shadows, their footsteps silent, their weapons ready. Nanny led her group toward the British camp, her senses attuned to every sound and movement around her.

As they approached, the glow of campfires became visible through the trees. The British soldiers laughed and talked, their confidence evident. They had no idea that the forest was watching.

Nanny raised a hand, signaling her warriors to halt. She crouched low, studying the camp's layout. The engineers' equipment was piled near the center, guarded by a handful of soldiers. Nearby, crates of supplies were stacked high, likely containing tools and ammunition.

"Ama's group will take the northern flank," she whispered to Kojo. "We'll target the equipment. Once the fires start, they'll scatter. Be ready to cover our retreat."

Kojo nodded and slipped into the shadows. Nanny signaled to her group, and they moved closer, their steps as silent as the wind.

The attack began with a single arrow, its tip alight with flame. It arced through the night, landing among the wooden crates. In seconds, the fire spread, consuming the supplies and casting flickering shadows across the camp.

Shouts of alarm erupted as soldiers scrambled to extinguish the flames. Nanny and her warriors struck swiftly, disabling equipment and cutting through ropes and chains. The chaos worked in their favor, the British too disoriented to mount an effective defense.

Nanny moved like a shadow, her spear flashing in the firelight. She struck with precision, each movement calculated to cause maximum damage. Around her, the Maroons fought with the same relentless determination, their unity unshakable.

As the fire spread, the forest seemed to come alive. Traps set earlier by Ama's group caught fleeing soldiers, and the dense foliage swallowed others whole. The British's confidence melted away, replaced by fear and confusion.

By the time the first light of dawn touched the treetops, the British camp was in ruins. The engineers' equipment lay shattered, their supplies reduced to ashes. Nanny regrouped with her warriors at a prearranged meeting point, their faces a mix of exhaustion and triumph.

Kojo approached her, a rare smile breaking through his usually serious demeanor. "We did it," he said. "They'll think twice before trying to tame this forest again."

Nanny nodded, her expression steady. "This is just one battle, Kojo. They'll be back, and we must be ready. But for now, we've shown them that this land will not bow to their will."

As the group made their way back to the village, the forest seemed to hum with approval. The fight for freedom was far from over, but the Maroons had proven once again that they were a force the British could not conquer. Together, they would protect their home, their people, and their future.

Chapter 9
Echoes of Resistance

The Maroon village buzzed with activity as news of the successful raid spread. Children ran between huts, mimicking warriors with makeshift spears, while the elders sat in circles, their words filled with pride and caution. The British had suffered a devastating blow, but Nanny knew this victory was just another chapter in a long, arduous struggle.

By the firelight that evening, Nanny gathered the warriors who had returned. Their faces were marked with exhaustion, their bodies bearing the scars of the night's battle, but their eyes burned with resolve.

"We've won today," Nanny began, her voice carrying across the gathering. "But this victory has sown seeds of vengeance in our enemies. The British will come back, stronger and more determined. We must not grow complacent."

Kojo stepped forward, his face serious. "What's our next move, Nanny? They won't stop until they believe us broken."

Nanny nodded, her expression thoughtful. "We need to solidify our alliances with other Maroon settlements. If the British mean to press harder, we must be ready to meet them as one. United, we are stronger than their guns and cannons."

Kwame, standing among the warriors, spoke up. "I can go. I owe this village a debt, and I will do what it takes to repay it."

Nanny regarded him for a long moment, then nodded. "You'll take a group of our best scouts and travel to the northern settlements. Deliver our message and learn what you can about their movements. Kojo and I will stay to prepare the village and strengthen our defenses."

The next morning, Kwame and his group set off, disappearing into the forest like shadows. Nanny watched them go, her heart heavy with the weight of the responsibility she had placed on their shoulders. Turning to Kojo, she motioned for him to follow her to the edge of the village, where the land sloped gently into a series of ridges.

"This is where they'll come next," she said, gesturing to the open terrain. "If they build their roads through here, they'll have a clear path to us. We need to make this land inhospitable."

Kojo frowned. "The terrain works against us. There's little cover, and their artillery will tear through any defenses we build."

"Then we won't build," Nanny replied. "We'll use what's already here. The earth itself will fight for us."

Over the following days, the Maroons transformed the landscape. Trenches were dug and concealed, false trails were laid to mislead the enemy, and shallow pits were filled with sharpened stakes and covered with foliage. The ridges became a labyrinth, a deadly maze designed to confuse and slow the British forces.

Meanwhile, Kwame's journey to the northern settlements was fraught with its own challenges. The forest, though familiar, was vast and treacherous. He and his team moved with caution, their senses attuned to every rustle of leaves and snap of twigs. They avoided British patrols, relying on their knowledge of the land to stay hidden.

When they reached the first settlement, they were greeted with cautious optimism. The northern Maroons had heard of Nanny's victories and were eager to stand with her. Kwame relayed her message, his voice steady and filled with conviction.

"The British are coming with everything they have," he said. "But together, we can stop them. We must be ready to fight as one."

The northern leaders agreed, pledging their warriors and resources to the cause. Kwame's team moved swiftly to the next settlement, carrying the call for unity like a torch.

Back in the village, Nanny felt the pressure of time weighing heavily on her. The forest's whispers seemed louder now, as though the land itself was urging her to act. The traps were nearly complete, but her thoughts turned to the warriors she had sent north. Would they return in time? Would their alliances hold?

Kojo approached her one evening as she stood at the edge of the village, gazing out over the ridges. "You're worried," he said.

Nanny's lips curved into a faint smile. "I'd be a fool not to be. Every decision feels like a gamble, Kojo. One misstep could cost us everything."

"You've led us this far," Kojo said. "And we've followed because we believe in you. The forest believes in you. Don't forget that."

Nanny's gaze softened, and she nodded. "Thank you, Kojo. We'll need that belief in the days to come."

The forest seemed to hold its breath as the Maroons awaited Kwame's return. When he finally emerged from the trees, his group trailing behind him, the village erupted in relief. He brought not only news of alliances but also scouts from the northern settlements, their presence a tangible sign of solidarity.

Nanny welcomed them with open arms, her heart swelling with pride and hope. "You've done well, Kwame. The northern Maroons stand with us, and together, we'll show the British that this land will never be theirs."

As night fell, the village gathered to prepare for the battle they knew was coming. Nanny stood before them, her voice steady and strong.

"We fight not just for ourselves but for every soul who dreams of freedom," she said. "The British may outnumber us, but they do not know this land like we do. They do not know our hearts. Together, we will show them the strength of a people who refuse to be broken."

The Maroons raised their voices in a chorus of defiance, their unity unshakable. The echoes of their resistance carried through the forest, a promise to their enemies and a testament to their resolve.

The battle ahead would be fierce, but Nanny knew one truth above all: the Maroons would endure, as they always had, together.

Chapter 10

The First Thunder

The storm began to build long before the first raindrop fell. The forest's usual hum was muted, replaced by a tense stillness that seemed to mirror the Maroons' anticipation. Nanny stood on the ridge overlooking the labyrinth they had created, her spear in hand. The air was heavy, charged with the electricity of an approaching storm—both from the skies and from the British forces gathering in the distance.

Kwame and Kojo joined her, their faces reflecting the same determination she felt.

"The scouts report the British are a day away," Kojo said. "They're moving cautiously but steadily. They'll reach the ridges by sunrise."

Nanny nodded, her eyes scanning the terrain. "Good. Let them come. The land will slow them, and when they're at their most vulnerable, we will strike."

Kwame shifted uneasily. "They'll have artillery, Nanny. If they make it past the ridges, our village…"

"They won't make it past," Nanny said firmly, her voice leaving no room for doubt. "We've prepared for this moment. Trust in the land, and trust in each other."

As night fell, the Maroons took their positions. The labyrinth of trenches and traps stretched across the ridges, a masterpiece of defensive ingenuity. Warriors crouched in concealed positions, their weapons at the ready. Nanny moved among them, offering words of encouragement and ensuring every detail was in place.

"Remember," she told them, "this land is our ally. Use it. Let the forest hide you, let the ridges protect you. Strike fast, then disappear. Confuse them. Make them fear the shadows."

The warriors nodded, their faces a mix of determination and tension. Nanny knew the fear in their eyes but also the fire. They had faced impossible odds before, and they would do so again.

The first light of dawn revealed the advancing British forces. The Redcoats moved cautiously, their bright uniforms stark against the muted greens and browns of the forest. Cannons rumbled on makeshift wheels, dragged laboriously through the uneven terrain. Officers barked orders, their voices carrying over the distance.

Nanny watched from her vantage point, her grip tightening on her spear. "Wait," she murmured to herself, her heart pounding. "Let them come closer."

The British reached the outer edge of the ridges, their formation tightening as the terrain grew more treacherous. Then, with a signal from Nanny, the Maroons struck.

The attack was swift and devastating. Arrows rained down from the trees, finding their marks with deadly precision. Warriors emerged from concealed trenches, striking and retreating before the Redcoats could react. The forest came alive with the sounds of battle—the clash of steel, the thud of musket fire, the cries of soldiers caught in traps.

The British attempted to regroup, their cannons firing blindly into the trees. But the Maroons were relentless, their knowledge of the terrain giving them an unassailable advantage. The labyrinth turned the enemy's strength against them, funneling them into chokepoints where they were ambushed and overwhelmed.

Nanny fought at the forefront, her spear a blur of motion. She moved like a shadow, her strikes precise and deadly. Around her, the Maroons pressed their advantage, their unity unshakable.

By midday, the battle had turned into a rout. The British, battered and demoralized, began to retreat, their artillery abandoned in the chaos. The forest, once again, had proven to be an impenetrable ally.

As the last of the Redcoats disappeared into the distance, a cheer rose from the Maroon warriors. Nanny stood among them, her spear planted firmly in the ground. Her heart swelled with pride, but she knew the fight was far from over.

Kojo approached her, his face streaked with sweat and dirt. "We did it," he said, his voice filled with awe. "We held them off."

Nanny nodded, her expression resolute. "This is just the beginning, Kojo. They will return, and when they do, we must be ready. But today, we've shown them that this land belongs to us."

That evening, the village celebrated their victory. Fires burned brightly, and songs of defiance echoed through the forest. Nanny sat quietly at the edge of the gathering, her gaze fixed on the flames. Kojo joined her, a rare smile on his face.

"You should celebrate," he said. "This victory is yours as much as anyone's."

Nanny shook her head. "This victory belongs to all of us, Kojo. The land, the people, the spirits of our ancestors. We fight together, and together we endure."

Kojo nodded, his smile fading into a look of respect. "And together, we will win."

As the celebration continued, Nanny allowed herself a moment of peace. The battle had been won, but the war for freedom was far from over. She knew the challenges ahead would be even greater, but she also knew the strength of her people. Together, they would face whatever came their way.

The first thunder of the storm rolled across the sky, a promise of rain and renewal. Nanny lifted her head, her eyes shining with determination. The Maroons had weathered the storm before, and they would do so again. For freedom. For their land. For their future.

Chapter 11
The Gathering Clouds

The morning after their victory, the forest seemed to hum with quiet satisfaction. The Maroon village awoke to the mingled scents of smoldering firewood and the damp earth, a reminder of the battle they had won and the land they continued to protect. Yet, as Nanny gazed over the horizon from her usual perch on the ridge, she felt a familiar weight settle in her chest. The British retreat was not an end but a prelude.

Kojo joined her, his steps heavy with the weariness of the previous day. He carried a small bundle of provisions and a roll of maps.

"You're thinking ahead," he said, laying the maps down. "Planning for the next move."

Nanny nodded, her eyes scanning the distant hills. "The British will return, Kojo. And next time, they will be prepared for the forest. We need to do more than defend. We must outmaneuver them, strike before they gather their strength."

Kojo studied the maps, tracing the lines of rivers and ridges. "The northern Maroons have pledged their warriors, but their forces are still days away. If we move too soon, we risk dividing our strength."

Nanny's gaze shifted to the village below. Children played in the clearing, their laughter a balm against the tension. "And if we wait too long, we give the British the upper hand. They will use the delay to reinforce and devise new strategies."

Kojo was silent for a moment, then nodded. "What do you propose?"

"We take the fight to them," Nanny said. "A series of swift, coordinated strikes to keep them off balance. We target their supply lines, disrupt their movements, and force them to divide their forces. Let them chase shadows while we strengthen our alliances."

The council convened that afternoon under the sprawling branches of the silk cotton tree. The warriors and elders listened intently as Nanny laid out her plan, her voice calm but commanding.

"We cannot wait for the British to come to us," she said. "We will take the offensive, using the forest to our advantage. Kojo will lead a team to the southern outposts, where the British are amassing supplies. Kwame, you will go north to coordinate with the arriving warriors and secure their commitment."

Kwame nodded, his face a mix of pride and determination. "What of you, Nanny?"

"I will lead a third team to disrupt their communication routes," she replied. "Without orders, their forces will falter. This will buy us the time we need to prepare for their eventual assault."

The council murmured their agreement, though the tension in the air was palpable. The risks were great, but the stakes were higher. They all knew the cost of failure.

As the sun dipped below the horizon, the Maroons prepared for their missions. Nanny moved among the warriors, her presence a steadying force. She offered words of encouragement, her voice carrying the weight of her unwavering belief in their cause.

"Every step we take, every strike we make, is for our freedom," she said. "The British may have their weapons and their numbers, but we have something far greater: our unity, our knowledge of this land, and our unbreakable spirit. Together, we will endure."

The warriors nodded, their resolve mirrored in their leader's words. Nanny's strength was their strength, her determination their beacon.

The forest embraced them as they set out under the cover of darkness. Nanny's team moved like shadows, their steps silent on the soft earth. The sounds of the night—the rustle of leaves, the distant call of an owl—were a familiar symphony, a reminder that the land was their ally.

As they neared the British communication route, Nanny signaled for her team to halt. She crouched low, her eyes scanning the area. A small outpost lay ahead, its campfires casting flickering light on the surrounding trees. Soldiers milled about, their movements lax with the false sense of security.

Nanny turned to her team, her voice barely a whisper. "We strike swiftly and silently. Take out their equipment and retreat before they can organize a counterattack. No unnecessary risks."

The warriors nodded, their weapons at the ready. With a wave of her hand, Nanny led them forward, the forest swallowing their movements.

The attack was executed with precision. Arrows flew through the night, extinguishing the campfires and plunging the outpost into chaos. Nanny's team moved with practiced efficiency, disabling communication lines and scattering the British's supplies. By the time the soldiers realized what was happening, the Maroons had vanished into the trees.

Nanny paused at the edge of the clearing, her heart pounding. The mission had gone as planned, but she knew this was only the beginning.

The British would soon realize the scale of their resistance, and their response would be swift and ruthless.

By the time they returned to the village, the first light of dawn was breaking. Nanny's team was greeted with quiet relief and gratitude. Kojo's group had also returned, reporting a successful raid on the southern outposts. Kwame's mission, however, remained ongoing.

Nanny stood at the center of the village, her gaze sweeping over her people. "We have struck a blow against the British, but our fight is far from over. We must remain vigilant, united, and unwavering. Together, we will face whatever comes our way."

The Maroons raised their voices in agreement, their unity unshakable. As the sun climbed higher, Nanny allowed herself a moment of quiet reflection. The storm was far from over, but she knew they had the strength to weather it. Together, they would endure. Together, they would prevail.

Chapter 12
Flames of Retaliation

The forest felt heavier in the days that followed. The air carried a tension that seemed to seep into the soil, the trees, and the hearts of the Maroons. Though their coordinated strikes had disrupted the British's plans, Nanny knew the enemy would not remain idle for long. The reprisal, when it came, would be swift and brutal.

Kwame returned to the village late one evening, his face drawn with exhaustion. He carried news from the northern settlements, where the Maroons were rallying their forces.

"They're ready to join us," he said, his voice hoarse but resolute. "Their warriors are on the move. But Nanny, the British…they've brought reinforcements. Ships have docked on the eastern coast, and their numbers are swelling."

Nanny's jaw tightened. The British's determination to crush the Maroon resistance was clear. But so was her resolve.

"Then we must prepare," she said. "We will meet them not with fear, but with fire."

The council gathered under the silk cotton tree, their faces illuminated by the flickering light of torches. Nanny stood before them, her presence commanding as always.

"The British are coming in greater numbers," she said. "They mean to destroy us, to take our land and our freedom. But they do not know the strength of this forest, or the strength of its people. We will fight them with every weapon we have, and we will show them that this land is not theirs to take."

Kojo stepped forward, his voice steady. "What's the plan, Nanny?"

"We strike first," she replied. "Their reinforcements will come through the eastern valleys. We'll set traps along their path, using fire to drive them into the heart of the forest. Once they're disoriented, we attack from all sides. Divide them, confuse them, and force them to retreat."

The council murmured their agreement, their resolve hardening with every word. The Maroons were no strangers to impossible odds, and Nanny's leadership had carried them through before.

As dawn broke, the Maroons set to work. Warriors moved silently through the forest, laying traps and gathering materials for the fires. The land itself became a weapon, its secrets and shadows wielded by those who knew it best.

Nanny led her people with tireless energy, her presence a source of strength. She worked alongside the youngest and the oldest, her hands as skilled with tools as they were with weapons. Her words carried a quiet determination that inspired all who heard them.

"This forest is alive," she said to a group of young warriors as they dug concealed trenches. "It breathes with us, fights with us. Trust it, and it will protect you."

The British forces arrived in the eastern valleys under the midday sun. Their columns stretched long and wide, their numbers bolstered by fresh reinforcements. Cannons rumbled on carts, and soldiers marched with an air of grim determination. But as they entered the dense forest, their confidence began to waver.

The first trap was triggered by a soldier's careless step. A hidden pit opened beneath him, swallowing him and sending panic rippling through the ranks. Arrows rained down from unseen heights, and the forest seemed to close in around them.

Then the fires began.

Flames erupted along the edges of the valley, consuming the dry brush and creating a wall of heat and smoke. The British soldiers coughed and stumbled, their formation breaking as they tried to escape the inferno. The Maroons struck swiftly, emerging from the shadows to unleash their fury.

Nanny fought at the forefront, her spear a blur of motion. She moved like a phantom, her strikes precise and devastating. Around her, the Maroons pressed their advantage, their unity and knowledge of the terrain turning the battle in their favor.

By nightfall, the British forces were in disarray. Their cannons lay abandoned, their soldiers scattered and demoralized. The forest, once again, had proven to be an impenetrable fortress.

Nanny stood on a ridge overlooking the battlefield, her chest heaving with exhaustion. Kojo joined her, his face streaked with sweat and ash.

"We've driven them back," he said, his voice filled with awe. "But they'll come again. They always do."

Nanny nodded, her gaze fixed on the horizon. "Let them come. As long as we stand, this forest will stand. And as long as the forest stands, we will fight."

The village celebrated their victory with songs and stories, their voices carrying through the night. Yet, even in the midst of their joy, there was a solemn understanding that their fight was far from over.

Nanny sat quietly at the edge of the gathering, her spear resting beside her. She felt the weight of the battle, the weight of leadership, but also the unyielding strength of her people.

"This land is ours," she whispered to herself, her voice resolute. "And we will never let it go."

The forest, their eternal ally, seemed to echo her words. Together, they would endure whatever storms lay ahead. Together, they would prevail.

Chapter 13
The Unseen Threat

The days following the fiery battle brought an uneasy calm to the Maroon village. The forest, their ally and fortress, seemed to breathe a sigh of relief, but Nanny knew better than to trust the quiet. The British had been driven back, but they would not stay away for long. Their pride was wounded, and a wounded enemy was a dangerous one.

Nanny stood at the edge of the village, her gaze fixed on the distant ridges. The morning mist clung to the trees, obscuring the horizon. Beside her, Kojo shifted uneasily, his hand resting on the hilt of his machete.

"The scouts haven't returned," he said, his voice low. "It's been two days. Something isn't right."

Nanny nodded, her expression unreadable. "The British are changing their tactics. They know they can't face us here, not without paying a heavy price. They'll try to weaken us from within."

Kojo frowned. "Sabotage?"

"Or betrayal," Nanny said, her voice laced with a quiet anger. "We must be vigilant. Call the council. We need to discuss our next move."

The council convened quickly, their faces shadowed with concern. Nanny addressed them with her usual calm authority, though her words carried a sharper edge than usual.

"The British are regrouping, but they're also watching us," she said. "They'll seek to exploit our weaknesses, to find cracks in our unity. We must close those cracks before they can break us apart."

Kwame, who had proven himself through his earlier missions, leaned forward. "Do you think they've turned someone in the village?"

Nanny's gaze swept over the council. "It's possible. Fear can be a powerful weapon, and the British know how to use it. But we cannot act on suspicion alone. We need information. Kojo, I want you to organize patrols. Watch for anything unusual. Kwame, take a small team and find the missing scouts. They may have encountered something we need to know."

The men nodded, their expressions grim. Nanny continued, her voice steady. "Above all, we must stay united. The British will do everything they can to divide us, but if we stand together, they cannot break us."

Kwame set out that afternoon with a group of trusted warriors. They moved swiftly through the forest, their senses attuned to every sound. The absence of the scouts weighed heavily on them, the silence of the forest unsettling.

By nightfall, they found the first sign of trouble. A broken arrow lay on the ground, its shaft splintered. Nearby, the underbrush was disturbed, as though a struggle had taken place. Kwame knelt to examine the ground, his jaw tightening.

"They were ambushed," he said. "But by who?"

The answer came moments later. A rustling in the trees drew their attention, and before they could react, a figure stumbled into the clearing. It was one of the scouts, his face pale and his clothing torn. He collapsed to the ground, gasping for breath.

"The British," he managed, his voice barely audible. "They've set traps…they're waiting for us."

Kwame's heart sank, but he forced himself to stay calm. "Where?"

"Near the river," the scout whispered. "They…they know our routes. Someone told them."

Back at the village, Nanny listened intently as Kwame relayed the scout's words. Her expression hardened with each detail, her mind racing.

"If they know our routes, they've been watching us closely," she said. "And if someone has been feeding them information…"

Kojo's jaw clenched. "We'll find the traitor, Nanny. Whoever it is won't get away with this."

"We will," Nanny agreed. "But we must be careful. Acting too quickly could push them deeper into hiding. For now, we focus on securing the village and protecting our people."

She turned to Kwame. "Double the patrols near the river. Set traps of our own. If the British mean to strike, we'll be ready for them."

Kwame nodded, his resolve clear. "We'll make sure they don't get the upper hand."

As the village prepared for the next confrontation, Nanny found herself walking through the forest alone. The trees, so familiar and comforting, now seemed to hold secrets in their shadows. She paused by a stream, the water's gentle murmur a stark contrast to the storm brewing in her mind.

"Spirits of the land," she whispered, "guide us. Protect us. Show us the truth."

The wind stirred the leaves, carrying her words into the depths of the forest. Nanny closed her eyes, drawing strength from the land she had sworn to protect. The British might have their spies and their weapons, but they did not have the spirit of the Maroons. They did not have the forest.

As she made her way back to the village, a single thought burned in her mind: no matter the cost, they would uncover the traitor. And when the British came again, they would be met with the full force of a people united, unbroken, and unyielding.

Chapter 14
The Trial Within

The Maroon village was restless. The scout's revelation of a possible traitor among them had cast a shadow over their hard-won unity. Nanny moved through the village with her usual composure, but the tension in the air was palpable. People spoke in hushed tones, their eyes darting suspiciously toward one another. Fear had begun to creep into their sanctuary.

At the council meeting that evening, the mood was heavy. Nanny stood at the center of the circle, her spear in hand, her gaze steady.

"We face two enemies," she began, her voice calm but firm. "The British, who threaten us from the outside, and fear, which threatens to divide us from within. If we are to survive, we must address both."

Kojo stepped forward, his expression hard. "The scout said someone's been feeding the British information. If that's true, we can't ignore it. We need to find the traitor."

Nanny nodded. "We will. But we will do so with care. Accusations without proof will only weaken us. Kwame, have the patrols noticed anything unusual?"

Kwame shook his head. "Nothing yet, but we've doubled our watches near the river and other key points. If someone tries to leave the village or signal the British, we'll catch them."

"Good," Nanny said. "In the meantime, we must continue our preparations. The British will not wait for us to solve this. We must be ready for whatever comes."

The following days were a mix of tense vigilance and tireless work. The Maroons fortified their defenses, laid new traps, and practiced their strategies. Nanny moved among her people, offering guidance and reassurance. She could see the strain on their faces, the way suspicion was beginning to take root. It pained her to see the trust they had built eroding, but she knew it was a battle they had to fight together.

One evening, as the sun dipped below the horizon, Kwame approached Nanny. His expression was troubled.

"There's been movement near the northern edge of the forest," he said. "Tracks that lead away from the village. They're fresh."

Nanny's eyes narrowed. "Show me."

Kwame led her to the edge of the forest, where faint footprints marked the soft earth. Nanny crouched, studying the tracks closely. They were deliberate, careful, as though the person making them had tried to avoid detection.

"These aren't random," she said. "Someone's been moving through here with purpose. We need to follow these tracks and see where they lead."

Nanny, Kwame, and a small group of trusted warriors moved through the forest, their steps silent as shadows. The tracks wound deeper into the trees, leading them toward a secluded clearing. There, they found a small cache of supplies: food, clothing, and a rolled-up map of the village's defenses.

Kwame's jaw tightened. "This is proof. Someone's been planning to betray us."

Nanny picked up the map, her heart heavy. The handwriting was unfamiliar, but the details it contained were damning. She looked around the clearing, her mind racing. Whoever had left these supplies here was still out there, and they would have to act quickly to prevent further damage.

"We take this back to the council," she said. "And we increase our patrols. Whoever this is, they're working against us, and we need to stop them before they do more harm."

Back at the village, the discovery of the cache sent shockwaves through the community. The council met late into the night, their voices low and serious as they discussed their next steps. Nanny listened carefully, her mind focused on the path ahead.

"We must be cautious," she said. "This traitor is dangerous, but fear and distrust will harm us just as much. We need to find them without tearing ourselves apart."

Kojo nodded. "What's the plan?"

"We lay a trap of our own," Nanny replied. "We use the cache to lure them out. Whoever comes back for it will reveal themselves. In the meantime, we continue to prepare for the British. They will not wait for us to solve this."

The council agreed, their resolve renewed. The village's strength lay in its unity, and they would not let a single betrayal destroy it.

As the trap was set and the Maroons returned to their work, Nanny stood at the edge of the forest, her spear in hand. The moonlight filtered through the trees, casting long shadows on the ground. She closed her eyes, reaching out to the spirits of the land for guidance.

"We will find the truth," she whispered. "And we will protect this village, no matter the cost."

The forest seemed to answer her, the rustling leaves and distant calls of the night creatures a quiet affirmation. Nanny opened her eyes, her resolve unshakable. The battle within was as critical as the one outside, and she would face it with the same strength and determination that had carried her this far.

Together, the Maroons would endure. Together, they would prevail.

Chapter 15

Shadows Unanswered

The cache remained untouched. Days turned to weeks, and still, no one returned to claim the bait. The Maroons, ever vigilant, kept their watch but began to grow restless. Nanny stood on the ridge overlooking the village, her spear by her side, her thoughts heavy with questions.

The Maroon village was a sanctuary, a haven for those who had escaped the chains of slavery and oppression. Its people were a patchwork of histories and heritages: warriors from the Ashanti Empire, farmers from the Congo, artisans from the Yoruba lands, and others whose ancestral names had been stripped from them but whose spirits remained unbroken. These men and women had forged a new identity here, bound not by blood but by the shared struggle for freedom.

It was this unity that made the notion of betrayal so perplexing to Nanny. To betray the Maroons was to betray not only one's people but also the hope and resilience that had sustained them. And yet, someone had whispered their secrets to the British. Someone had tried to fracture the foundation they had built together.

Kojo approached, his expression as troubled as her thoughts. "No sign of movement near the cache," he said. "Whoever it was, they've gone silent."

Nanny nodded, her gaze fixed on the horizon. "The silence is a strategy. Either they're waiting for us to let our guard down, or the threat is deeper than we thought."

"You think it's more than one person?" Kojo asked.

"I think desperation can spread like a disease," Nanny replied. "The British offer lies dressed as promises. Freedom for one's family. Safety from harm. It's a poison they've used before, and they will use it again."

Kojo sighed, his frustration evident. "The Maroons are strong, united. How could someone believe their lies?"

"Fear makes people forget who they are," Nanny said quietly. "But it is up to us to remind them. We must remain vigilant, not just against the British but against the seeds of doubt they plant."

The story of the Maroons was one of resilience born from pain. Many had arrived in Jamaica as slaves, torn from their homelands and forced into labor. Others were the children of those who had escaped, their memories of the old world passed down in stories and songs. Together, they had carved out a life in the mountains, turning the dense forests and steep ridges into fortresses against their oppressors.

In the village, the elders told these stories to the children, ensuring the lessons of their past were never forgotten. "We come from many places," one elder said, her voice strong despite her age. "But here, we are one people. Never forget that."

Nanny listened from the edge of the gathering, her heart heavy. The unity of the Maroons was their greatest strength, but it was also their greatest vulnerability. If the British could fracture that unity, they would win without firing a shot.

As the days passed, Nanny's unease grew. The lack of movement around the cache was troubling, but it was the silence within the village that concerned her more. Whispers of suspicion had begun to circulate, subtle but dangerous.

Kwame approached her one evening, his expression serious. "People are starting to look over their shoulders," he said. "They're questioning each other. It's small now, but it could grow."

"We need to address it," Nanny said. "Bring the council together. We must remind the village of who we are and what we fight for."

That night, the council met under the sprawling branches of the silk cotton tree. Nanny stood before them, her spear planted firmly in the ground.

"The British seek to destroy us not just with their weapons, but with their whispers," she began. "They want us to turn on each other, to doubt the bonds that hold us together. But we must not let them. Our strength is in our unity, in the knowledge that we fight not as individuals, but as one people."

The council nodded, their resolve mirrored in their leader's words. Nanny continued, her voice steady.

"We will not act on suspicion alone. We will not let fear guide our actions. Instead, we will fortify our defenses, strengthen our alliances, and trust in the forest and in each other. If a threat remains among us, it will reveal itself in time. Until then, we stand together."

The council's agreement was unanimous. The Maroons would not let the British's lies divide them. They would face whatever came their way, united and unbroken.

As the village returned to its preparations, Nanny stood alone at the edge of the forest, reminiscing a time of peace and happiness.

Chapter 16

Memories of Home

The sound of the forest faded as Nanny stood at the edge of the ridge, her gaze lost in the distant horizon. Her spear rested by her side, forgotten for the moment as her mind traveled to a time long past—a time of peace, when she lived as the daughter of royalty in her homeland.

She closed her eyes, and the memories came rushing back like the tide.

The courtyard was alive with the sounds of practice. Young warriors-in-training sparred with wooden staffs while elders observed, their voices carrying wisdom and advice. Nanny's father, the king, stood at the center of it all, his commanding presence unmatched. Clad in a flowing robe of deep indigo adorned with gold embroidery, he watched her approach with a smile that softened his otherwise stern features.

"Come, Nanny," he called, his voice carrying over the sounds of clashing wood. "Today, you learn more than words and rules. Today, you learn to defend."

She hesitated for only a moment before hurrying to him. Though she was young, barely old enough to wield a staff, her heart swelled with pride at the thought of training alongside the warriors. Her father handed her a smaller, intricately carved staff, its weight unfamiliar in her hands.

"Hold it firm," he instructed, guiding her stance. "Your weapon is an extension of yourself. It must flow with your movements, not fight against them."

Under his patient instruction, Nanny practiced the basics of combat. Her father's corrections were gentle but firm, his encouragement steady. "Again," he said, as she swung the staff awkwardly. "Do not fear mistakes. Fear not learning from them."

The session ended with her panting and covered in dust, but her father's approval made the effort worthwhile. "You have the spirit of a warrior, my daughter," he said, resting a hand on her shoulder. "And one day, that spirit will guide your people."

In the evenings, when the palace grew quiet, Nanny would sneak away to the edge of the village. There, her grandmother—a revered elder and keeper of ancient knowledge—lived in a modest hut surrounded by a garden of medicinal plants. The air around the hut was always thick with the aroma of herbs and the faint hum of chants.

"You're late, little one," her grandmother said one night, not turning from the mortar she was grinding. Her voice carried no reproach, only the warmth of familiarity.

"Father made me train longer," Nanny replied, seating herself cross-legged on the floor. "He says I must learn to defend."

"And he is right," her grandmother said, her hands never pausing. "But there are battles fought with more than weapons."

She handed Nanny a bundle of dried leaves. "Crush these. Feel their power. Each plant carries a spirit, a purpose. To know them is to wield a different kind of strength."

As the night deepened, her grandmother taught her the secrets of obeah, the ancient practices that connected them to the earth and their ancestors.

Nanny listened intently, her small hands mimicking her grandmother's deft movements.

"This knowledge is not for power alone," her grandmother said. "It is for balance. For healing. Remember, Nanny, a true leader knows when to strike and when to soothe."

The memories shifted, weaving together the lessons of her father and grandmother. Her father's strength, his belief in discipline and unity, had shaped her sense of duty. Her grandmother's wisdom, her connection to the unseen, had deepened her understanding of resilience and purpose.

Nanny opened her eyes, the present rushing back to her. The ridge before her was no longer the vast plains of her homeland, but the mountains of Jamaica. Yet, the lessons remained, carried in her heart like a flame.

She picked up her spear, her grip firm and steady. The British did not understand the depth of her strength, the legacy she carried. But they would learn.

"We will endure," she whispered to the forest, her voice steady. "For the warriors, for the healers, for all who came before us."

Chapter 17

The Midnight Raid

The forest was alive with anticipation. The reinforcements from the other Maroon villages had arrived, their warriors blending seamlessly into the shadows of the trees. Nanny stood at the center of the gathered leaders, her spear in hand, her voice low but commanding as she laid out the final details of the attack.

"The British are overconfident," she said. "They believe their numbers and their firepower make them untouchable. Tonight, we show them the strength of unity and the power of the land they seek to conquer. Move swiftly, strike decisively, and let the forest shield you."

Kojo nodded, his face set with determination. "We'll split into three groups as planned. The first will target their munitions. The second will dismantle their artillery. The third, led by you, Nanny, will take out their command tent. Without their leaders, they'll fall into chaos."

Nanny's gaze swept over the warriors, her people, her family in arms. "This is not just a battle," she said. "It is a message. Let them know they will never own this land, and they will never break us."

The attack began under the cover of darkness, the moonlight filtering through the dense canopy. The Maroons moved like whispers in the wind, their footsteps silent on the forest floor. Nanny led her group toward the heart of the British camp, where the command tent stood surrounded by guards.

The first sign of the attack came with the sudden, muted explosions of the munitions depot. Flames leaped into the sky, illuminating the camp and throwing the soldiers into disarray. Shouts filled the air as the British scrambled to extinguish the fires and defend their positions.

Kojo's group struck next, descending on the artillery with precision. Using tools they had brought with them, they dismantled the cannons and destroyed the wheels, rendering the British's heavy firepower useless. The sound of snapping wood and clashing steel blended with the chaos of the burning depot.

Nanny and her team reached the command tent as the camp plunged deeper into confusion. The guards, distracted by the fires, were quickly and silently dispatched. Nanny slipped inside the tent, her spear poised, her eyes scanning the room.

The British officers, caught off guard, barely had time to react. Nanny moved with the precision of a predator, her spear striking true as her warriors followed her lead. Papers and maps lay strewn across the table, the British's plans laid bare. Nanny's piercing gaze landed on a map spread across the British table, its intricate markings so precise it seemed to breathe life into the parchment. The goat skin bore every trail, every stream, every crevice of their village, rendered with a skill that sent a chill down her spine. Without hesitation, she seized the map and thrust it into the flames, her jaw set with determination. As the edges curled and blackened in the fire, she turned to her team, her voice low but commanding. "Burn the rest," she ordered, the urgency in her tone leaving no room for questions. The papers disappeared into the flames, their secrets consumed before they could become weapons in the hands of their enemies.

As they exited the tent, more warriors joined the fray, their coordinated strikes driving the British further into chaos. Arrows rained from the trees, finding their marks with deadly accuracy. The forest seemed to come alive, its shadows concealing the Maroons and amplifying the fear of their enemies.

The battle raged for what felt like hours but was, in truth, only a matter of minutes. The British, overwhelmed and unable to regroup, began to retreat. Their shouts of retreat mingled with the cries of the wounded and the roar of the flames.

By the time the first light of dawn crept over the horizon, the British camp was in ruins. Their munitions destroyed, their artillery dismantled, and their command structure shattered, they fled into the forest, their confidence as broken as their weapons.

The Maroons gathered at a prearranged clearing, their faces lit with the quiet pride of victory. Nanny stood before them, her spear planted firmly in the ground, her voice steady as she addressed her people.

"This is what unity can achieve," she said. "Together, we have shown them the strength of a people who refuse to be conquered. They will return, but so will we. Stronger. Smarter. Always united."

The warriors raised their weapons in silent agreement, their resolve unshaken. The forest around them seemed to hum with approval, a living testament to their resilience.

As the group dispersed to return to their villages, Nanny lingered, her gaze fixed on the horizon. The battle had been won, but the war for freedom was far from over. Yet, in the faces of her warriors and the strength of their unity, she saw hope—hope that no matter the cost, they would endure.

The forest, their eternal ally, whispered its agreement. Together, they would rise above every challenge. Together, they would prevail.

Chapter 18

The Aftermath of Flames

The sun rose slowly over the ruins of the British camp, its golden rays cutting through the lingering smoke and ash. Nanny and her warriors had returned to their hidden paths in the forest, their movements swift and silent as they made their way back to the village. The victory was undeniable, but Nanny's mind was heavy with what she had seen—and destroyed—in the British command tent.

The map of their village had been unmistakable. Its details were precise, far too detailed for mere reconnaissance. The goat-skin document bore the marks of someone intimately familiar with the Maroon stronghold. A traitor was among them, and Nanny's worst fears were confirmed.

As her team reached the safety of the village outskirts, Kojo caught up to her, his brow furrowed. "Nanny, we need to debrief the council about the British's plans. Those maps…"

Nanny cut him off with a sharp glance. "The maps are gone," she said firmly. "They serve no purpose now but to divide us. What we focus on is strengthening our defenses and ensuring no one's loyalties waver."

Kojo hesitated but nodded. "You're right. But if they knew so much about the village, we must act quickly."

"We will," Nanny said, her tone leaving no room for doubt. "But this stays between us for now."

The village erupted in quiet celebration as the warriors returned. The elders sang songs of triumph, and the children darted between the gathered crowd, their faces alight with joy. For a moment, the shadow of the British threat seemed distant.

Nanny allowed herself a brief smile, but her thoughts remained elsewhere. She caught Kwame's eye and gestured for him and Kojo to follow her. Together, they made their way to the council circle, where the other leaders waited.

"The British camp is no more," Nanny began, her voice steady. "Their munitions destroyed, their command structure shattered. But this victory comes with a warning. They will return, and they will come better prepared."

Kwame nodded. "They fought hard, even in their confusion. Next time, they will not be so easily undone."

Nanny's gaze swept over the council. "We need to strengthen our defenses and expand our patrols. But there is another matter…" She hesitated, weighing her next words carefully. "The British knew too much about us. They had details of the village that no outsider should have. Someone, somewhere, has been feeding them information."

Gasps rippled through the group, but Nanny raised a hand to silence them. "We will not give in to suspicion or fear," she said. "Our unity is our strength, and we will not let it be broken. But we must be vigilant. Watch for anything unusual. Trust will be earned, not assumed."

The council agreed, though unease lingered in their expressions. Nanny dismissed them, knowing that the seeds of doubt, once planted, could grow if not carefully managed.

That night, Nanny sat alone near the edge of the village, her spear resting across her lap. The forest was alive with its usual symphony, but her mind was far from peaceful. She thought of the goat-skin map, its intricate markings burned into her memory. Someone had betrayed them, and until she uncovered who, every face in the village was a potential threat.

Her grandmother's voice echoed in her mind: "A leader must know when to strike and when to soothe." Nanny had struck, delivering a devastating blow to the British. Now, she needed to soothe the fractures within her own people before they widened.

Kojo's voice broke her reverie. "You're troubled," he said, stepping into the moonlight.

"I'm thinking," Nanny replied. "About what comes next. About how we keep this village safe when trust is at risk."

Kojo sat beside her, his expression serious. "The people believe in you, Nanny. They'll follow your lead."

"Belief is fragile," Nanny said softly. "And the British know how to exploit fragility. We must be stronger than their lies. Stronger than the doubts they've sown."

Kojo nodded, his respect for her evident. "We'll get through this. Together."

As the night deepened, Nanny remained by the forest's edge, her resolve hardening. The Maroons had faced impossible odds before and emerged victorious. They would do so again, but only if they remained united.

The forest whispered its agreement, the rustling leaves carrying its quiet promise. Together, they would endure. Together, they would prevail.

Chapter 19

The Journey to Moore Town

The sun cast long shadows over the forest as the Maroons began their journey deeper into the Blue Mountains. The air was heavy with the scent of earth and foliage, a constant reminder of the land they were fighting to protect. Nanny walked at the front of the procession, her spear in hand, her thoughts as focused as her steps. Behind her, families carried their few belongings, warriors guarded the flanks, and children whispered with curiosity about their new home.

The decision to move had not come easily. The Blue Mountains were vast and treacherous, offering both sanctuary and challenge. Their new settlement, Moore Town, was a place of promise, but it was also a place of negotiation. The Taino Maroons, who had lived in the area long before Nanny's arrival, were reluctant to share their land. It had taken days of careful dialogue to convince them that unity was their strongest weapon against the British.

"This land has protected us," one Taino elder had said, his voice filled with pride. "Allowing you to join us will only bring death."

"Bring death, bring death," Nanny thundered. We the Maroon bring hope; the British bring death." Nanny reminded them of the many times the Marron came to their rescue to fight off runaway slaves from raiding their fields and provide an escort to traverse the mountains.

Nanny had stood before them, her voice steady. "We do not come to take from you. We come to join you. Together, we can create a home that no enemy can touch. But divided, we will fall."

Her words, along with the respect she showed for their traditions, had swayed the Taino Maroons. They agreed to guide the newcomers to a fertile valley where they could build their settlement.

As they journeyed, Nanny's thoughts wandered back to her homeland. The memories came unbidden, vivid and bittersweet. She could almost hear the rhythmic drums of her village, smell the spices of her mother's cooking, and feel the warmth of her father's hand as he guided her through the palace gardens.

She remembered the evenings when her father would sit beneath the great baobab tree, his voice weaving tales of their ancestors. "Our strength lies in our unity," he would say. "A kingdom divided is no kingdom at all."

Her mother, the queen, had been equally formidable, her wisdom as sharp as her father's spear. She had taught Nanny the importance of compassion, of listening to her people, and of finding balance between power and mercy.

And then there was her sister, Sekesu. The two of them had been inseparable, their bond forged in laughter and shared dreams. Sekesu had always been the more impulsive one, her spirit unrestrained like the river that cut through their village. Nanny smiled faintly at the memory of Sekesu daring her to climb the highest tree in the garden, the two of them laughing breathlessly when they reached the top.

"We're nearing the valley," Kojo's voice broke through her reverie. He walked beside her, his expression a mix of caution and optimism. "The Taino scouts say the land is fertile and well-protected."

Nanny nodded. "Good. The people are tired, but they're resilient. Once we're settled, we'll fortify the area and plan our next steps."

Behind them, Sekesu walked among the children, her voice carrying as she told them stories of their ancestors. She had taken on the role of a guide and nurturer, her energy a balm for the weary travelers.

"Your sister has a gift," Kojo observed, glancing back. "She keeps the people's spirits high."

"She always has," Nanny said with a small smile. "Even in the darkest times."

By nightfall, they reached the valley. The Taino guides showed them the natural springs and fertile soil, the dense forest that would shield them from prying eyes. It was a place of promise, a sanctuary carved from the wilderness.

As the Maroons began to set up their temporary shelters, Nanny stood at the edge of the clearing, her eyes scanning the horizon. The journey had been long, but it was far from over. The British would not rest, and neither would she.

Sekesu approached, her hand resting lightly on Nanny's shoulder. "We're safe for now," she said. "But you're already planning the next move, aren't you?"

"Always," Nanny replied. "Safety is fleeting. Freedom is what we fight for."

The two sisters stood in silence, the weight of their shared responsibilities unspoken but understood. Together, they would guide their people through whatever storms lay ahead. Together, they would ensure that the Maroons not only survived but thrived.

Nanny turned to face the camp, her voice steady and resolute. "This is our home now," she said. "And we will defend it with everything we have. Let the British come. They will find no weakness here."

The forest seemed to echo her words, its whispers a quiet promise of solidarity. Together, they would endure. Together, they would prevail.

Chapter 20
A Glimpse of Peace

Moore Town had become a sanctuary, its people finding comfort in the fertile valley and the dense forest that protected them. For the first time in months, the Maroons felt a fragile sense of calm. The British seemed far away, their threats muffled by the towering Blue Mountains. In this rare moment of reprieve, Nanny found herself drawn to the quiet corners of the settlement, places where she could reflect and, unexpectedly, begin to feel something she hadn't allowed herself in years: companionship.

It began simply. A warrior named Adisa, one of the reinforcements who had joined from a neighboring Maroon village, caught her attention. He was not one to boast, but his actions spoke volumes. In battle, he was precise and fearless, his movements echoing the fluidity of the forest itself. In the village, he worked tirelessly, helping families build homes and teaching the younger warriors the strategies that had kept him alive.

One evening, as the sun dipped below the mountains, casting a golden glow over the valley, Nanny sat by a small stream, her spear resting beside her. The sound of the water was soothing, a reminder of life's quiet rhythms. She did not hear Adisa approach until he spoke.

"Even the strongest warrior needs a moment to rest," he said, his voice warm but respectful.

Nanny turned to see him standing a few steps away, his hands empty to show he meant no intrusion. She gestured for him to sit, her expression softening. "Rest is fleeting for those who lead," she replied. "There's always another battle, another decision to make."

Adisa nodded, settling beside her. "True. But even leaders need to remember what they're fighting for. Peace, family, freedom. Without those, the fight loses its meaning."

They spoke for hours, their conversation flowing as easily as the stream beside them. Adisa shared stories of his homeland, tales of his family, and the dreams he once held before the chains of slavery had brought him to Jamaica. Nanny, in turn, found herself sharing memories of her father's wisdom, her mother's compassion, and her sister Sekesu's unyielding spirit. It was rare for her to speak so openly, but something about Adisa's presence made her feel safe.

In the weeks that followed, their connection deepened. Adisa became a confidant, someone Nanny could trust amidst the burdens of leadership. He never sought to overshadow her authority, instead offering quiet support and counsel when needed. Together, they walked the perimeter of Moore Town, discussed strategies for defense, and even shared moments of laughter—a sound Nanny had almost forgotten.

One evening, as the village gathered around the fire for songs and stories, Adisa approached Nanny with a small bundle wrapped in cloth.

"For you," he said, placing it in her hands.

She unwrapped it carefully, revealing a delicate bracelet made of braided vines and small, polished stones. Each stone was etched with symbols from their shared African heritage.

"To remind you," Adisa said, "of where we come from and what we're building here."

Nanny's fingers traced the intricate designs, her heart swelling with an unfamiliar warmth. "Thank you," she said softly, slipping the bracelet onto her wrist. "I will cherish it."

For a brief moment, Nanny allowed herself to imagine a life beyond the struggle. She saw herself walking beside Adisa, not as a leader burdened by responsibility, but as a woman, free to dream and build a future. She saw children playing in the fields, laughter echoing through the valley, and a community thriving in the peace they had fought so hard to secure.

But the visions were fleeting, like the morning mist that vanished with the rising sun. Nanny knew the fight was far from over. The British were still out there, and the safety of Moore Town depended on vigilance and unity.

Yet, in those quiet moments with Adisa, she found a strength she hadn't known she needed. His presence reminded her that even amidst the chaos of war, there was room for love, for connection, for hope.

As the night deepened and the fire burned low, Nanny sat beside Adisa, her hand resting lightly on the bracelet he had given her. For the first time in what felt like an eternity, she allowed herself to believe that peace was possible—not just for her people, but for herself.

Chapter 21

Sisterly Counsel

The sun hung low over Moore Town, casting the village in a warm golden glow. The day's work was done, and the hum of evening life filled the air. Nanny found her sister Sekesu sitting on a log near the communal fire, weaving strands of dried grass into a sturdy rope. Her movements were deliberate, her focus sharp, but the familiar mischievous glint in her eyes told Nanny that she was open to conversation.

Nanny approached, her spear tucked under her arm. "Sekesu, I need your advice," she began, her tone measured.

Sekesu looked up, her brow lifting in exaggerated surprise. "Nanny, the great leader of the Maroons, asking me for advice? This must be serious."

Nanny rolled her eyes but couldn't suppress a small smile. "It is serious. It's about Adisa."

Sekesu's hands paused, and a slow grin spread across her face. "Oh, this is good. Go on, I'm listening."

Nanny sighed, seating herself beside her sister. "He mentioned… he mentioned wanting to marry me."

Sekesu's grin turned into a full-blown laugh. "Adisa? The tall, quiet one with the broad shoulders? Oh, Nanny, you've done well."

"This is exactly why I was hesitant to bring it up," Nanny muttered, though her lips twitched with amusement.

Sekesu leaned closer, her voice dropping to a conspiratorial whisper. "Well, what did you say?"

"I didn't say anything," Nanny admitted. "I changed the subject. I'm not... I don't know how to handle this. I've been leading, fighting, planning. Marriage wasn't exactly on my mind."

Sekesu smirked. "You mean to tell me you can outsmart the British but a man's proposal leaves you speechless?"

Nanny shot her a mock glare. "This is why I need your advice, not your jokes."

Sekesu set the rope aside and turned fully to face her sister. "Alright, let's talk about this seriously. Do you like him?"

Nanny hesitated, her fingers brushing against the bracelet Adisa had given her. "I do," she said quietly. "He's kind, strong, and thoughtful. And he understands the weight of what we're doing here."

Sekesu nodded. "Sounds like a good match. So what's stopping you?"

"I... I don't know if I can balance being a wife and a leader," Nanny admitted. "And part of me wonders if this is the right time for such things, with the British still a threat."

Sekesu leaned back, her expression thoughtful. "I can't tell you what to do, but I will say this: life doesn't wait for perfect timing. If you care for him, and he's willing to stand beside you in all of this, why not give it a chance?"

Nanny nodded slowly. "You're right. But it's still... complicated."

Sekesu's grin returned. "When has your life ever been simple, Nanny?"

They both laughed, the tension easing. After a moment, Sekesu's eyes gleamed with mischief. "Do you remember that boy back in our village? What was his name? The one who used to bring you flowers?"

Nanny groaned. "You mean Kofi? The one who fell out of the mango tree trying to impress me?"

Sekesu clapped her hands, laughing so hard tears formed in her eyes. "Yes! And you just walked away while he lay there groaning. Poor Kofi. You were ruthless even then."

"I wasn't ruthless," Nanny said, though she couldn't help but chuckle. "I just didn't have time for foolishness."

Sekesu shook her head, still laughing. "And yet, here we are. The fearless Nanny asking about love. If only Kofi could see you now."

Nanny shook her head but smiled. "Thank you, Sekesu. I needed this."

Sekesu reached over and squeezed her sister's hand. "Anytime. Just remember, you don't have to face everything alone. Whether it's the British or love, you've got people who care about you."

Nanny's smile softened. "I'll think about what you said. And Adisa."

Sekesu winked. "Good. And if you do decide to marry him, let me know. I'll make sure the whole village celebrates properly."

As the night deepened, the two sisters continued talking, their laughter echoing into the quiet of Moore Town. For the first time in a long while, Nanny felt the weight on her shoulders lighten, even if just for a moment.

Chapter 22
The Union of Hearts

The morning air was filled with a sense of anticipation. Moore Town buzzed with excitement, the villagers busy with preparations for a celebration unlike any they had seen before. Nanny, their fearless leader, had made her decision—she had accepted Adisa's proposal, and today, they would unite in marriage.

Nanny stood in her small hut, her sister Sekesu adjusting the delicate beadwork on her ceremonial dress. The gown, made of finely woven cotton, was adorned with symbols representing strength, unity, and prosperity. A crown of braided vines and wildflowers sat atop her head, and her wrist bore the bracelet Adisa had given her, its polished stones gleaming in the soft light.

"You look beautiful," Sekesu said, stepping back to admire her sister. "And powerful. As always."

Nanny gave her a small smile, her nerves showing despite her usual composure. "It feels... strange," she admitted. "I've spent so much of my life fighting and leading. I never imagined this for myself."

Sekesu placed a reassuring hand on her shoulder. "You deserve this, Nanny. Love and leadership aren't opposites. They can strengthen each other. Besides, Adisa is a good man. He'll stand by you in every battle, just as you've stood by our people."

Nanny nodded, drawing strength from her sister's words. "Thank you, Sekesu. For everything."

Sekesu grinned. "Don't get all sentimental on me now. We've got a wedding to attend."

The ceremony took place in the heart of the village, beneath the shade of a massive silk cotton tree. The entire community had gathered, their faces glowing with joy and pride. Children ran around, their laughter echoing through the valley, while elders sat in a semicircle, their eyes filled with wisdom and approval.

Adisa stood near the base of the tree, his posture calm but his eyes searching the crowd for Nanny. He was dressed in traditional attire, his tunic embroidered with patterns that matched Nanny's gown. Around his neck hung a carved pendant, a symbol of protection and honor.

When Nanny appeared, led by Sekesu, the crowd fell silent. She moved with her usual grace, her head held high, her presence commanding yet serene. Adisa's breath caught as their eyes met, a quiet understanding passing between them.

The ceremony was simple but profound. The village elder, a woman with silver-streaked hair and a voice that carried the weight of generations, spoke of unity and resilience. She reminded everyone that this union was not just a personal commitment but a symbol of the strength and hope that bound the Maroons together.

"Together, you are stronger," the elder said, her gaze shifting between Nanny and Adisa. "Your love will be a shield against despair and a light in the darkest times. As you lead, as you fight, remember this bond. It is your foundation."

Nanny and Adisa exchanged vows, their words simple but heartfelt. Nanny's voice was steady, her eyes unwavering as she spoke. "Adisa, you have shown me that even in the midst of war, there is room for love.

I promise to stand beside you, to lead with you, and to protect what we hold dear."

Adisa took her hands in his, his voice filled with quiet strength. "Nanny, you are the strongest person I have ever known. I promise to honor you, to fight for our people with you, and to cherish the peace we create together."

The elder tied their hands together with a braided cord, a symbol of their unity. The crowd erupted in cheers as the newlyweds turned to face their people, their smiles radiant.

The celebration that followed was filled with music, dancing, and laughter. The villagers feasted on roasted yams, fresh fruits, and spiced fish, their spirits high as they celebrated not only the marriage but the resilience of their community.

Sekesu pulled Nanny onto the makeshift dance floor, laughing as she spun her sister around. "See? You can fight and dance!" she teased.

Nanny laughed, a rare sound that warmed everyone who heard it. Adisa joined them, his movements confident as he took Nanny's hand and led her into a slower rhythm. For a moment, the world beyond Moore Town faded, and all that remained was joy.

As the night deepened and the celebration began to wind down, Nanny and Adisa stood at the edge of the village, gazing out at the stars. The forest was quiet, the air cool and fragrant.

"Are you ready for what comes next?" Adisa asked, his voice soft.

Nanny looked at him, her heart steady. "With you by my side, I am."

He reached for her hand, their fingers intertwining. Together, they stood in silence, their love a beacon in the dark, a promise of hope and strength for the battles yet to come.

Chapter 23

A Season of Peace

For the first time in what felt like an eternity, Moore Town thrived in peace. The British, nursing their wounds from repeated defeats, had grown hesitant to challenge the Maroons. This respite allowed the community to flourish. The dense forests surrounding the village provided natural protection, while the fertile valley yielded bountiful harvests that fed their growing population.

The Maroons, ever industrious, had turned their settlement into a bustling hub of activity. Fields of yam, cassava, corn, and squashstretched as far as the eye could see. Men hunted ducks and coney in the forests and fished in the nearby streams, their catches bringing variety to the community's meals. Women worked tirelessly, tending to the crops, weaving baskets, and preparing food, their songs harmonizing with the sounds of daily life. Markets sprung up, where people traded goods, shared stories, and celebrated their shared prosperity. Schools were built to teach the children not only survival skills but also the rich history of their people, ensuring the next generation would carry the torch of freedom.

In a quiet corner of the village, a small building served as a place of healing. Here, the sick and injured were cared for with herbal remedies and the knowledge passed down by the elders. It was a sanctuary of hope, where the Taino Maroons' wisdom blended seamlessly with African traditions.

Nanny watched this transformation with a deep sense of pride. Moore Town was more than a stronghold; it was a beacon of resilience and unity. And in the heart of it all, she found joy not just as a leader but as a mother.

Her three-year-old daughter, Ama, was a whirlwind of energy. The little girl darted between the villagers, her laughter echoing through the valley. She had inherited her mother's sharp eyes and her father's calm demeanor, a combination that made her both curious and fearless. Nanny often found herself chasing Ama through the fields, laughing as the child evaded her with surprising agility.

"You'll need all your strength for this one," Adisa teased one afternoon, watching from the porch of their home as Nanny tried in vain to scoop Ama into her arms.

"She's faster than a gazelle," Nanny replied, finally catching Ama and lifting her high into the air. "But no one escapes me for long."

Ama squealed with delight, her tiny arms wrapping around her mother's neck. Nanny held her close, her heart full of a happiness she hadn't thought possible.

The days passed peacefully, marked by the rhythms of life and the steady growth of the community. Nanny's second pregnancy was progressing well, and the elders, with their keen intuition, had already predicted the child's gender.

"It will be a boy," said Elder Kwame, his voice full of certainty. "Strong and brave, like his mother and father."

Sekesu, ever the joker, grinned. "I'll bet he'll have your stubbornness too, Nanny."

"If he does, it will serve him well," Nanny replied with a smirk. "This world is no place for the faint-hearted."

Despite her teasing, Sekesu had taken on the role of doting aunt with enthusiasm. She often played with Ama, telling her stories of their homeland and the ancestors who had paved the way for their freedom. Ama's wide-eyed wonder reminded everyone of the importance of passing down their history.

In the evenings, the village would gather around the fire to share meals and stories. Nanny, though usually focused on strategy and leadership, allowed herself to relax in these moments. With Ama nestled against her and Adisa's arm draped protectively around her shoulders, she felt a peace she hadn't known since her childhood.

"Do you think this peace will last?" Adisa asked one night, his voice low so as not to disturb Ama, who had fallen asleep in her lap.

Nanny glanced at the glowing embers of the fire, her expression thoughtful. "Peace is fragile, like a delicate plant. It needs constant tending. But as long as we stand together, I believe we can protect it."

Adisa nodded, his hand resting gently on hers. "Then we will protect it. For Ama, for the one yet to come, and for all those who look to us for strength."

Nanny leaned into him, her resolve steady. The future was uncertain, but in that moment, surrounded by her family and her people, she allowed herself to hope. Together, they had built something remarkable. Together, they would defend it.

As the stars glittered above Moore Town, the village slept peacefully, the sounds of the forest a gentle lullaby. Nanny's hand rested on her growing belly, a quiet promise forming in her heart. Her family, her people, her freedom—she would fight for them all, but tonight, she would simply cherish the gift of this peaceful season.

Chapter 24

Whispers of the Ancestors

The days of peace continued, the Maroon community thriving in the fertile embrace of the Blue Mountains. Yet, amidst the bustling activity of farming, teaching, and trade, Nanny began to sense something stirring in the quiet moments of her day. It was subtle at first: a rustling in the leaves when there was no wind, the feeling of being watched not by enemies but by something older, deeper.

One night, as the village gathered around the fire for stories, Nanny found herself staring into the flames, her mind drifting. The voices of her ancestors seemed to whisper on the edges of her consciousness, calling her to remember.

The call became undeniable during one of her routine walks through the forest. Nanny often took these walks to clear her mind, her spear in hand more out of habit than necessity. The dense canopy above shielded her from the sun, and the earthy scent of the forest grounded her. This time, however, she felt a pull, as though the forest itself was guiding her steps.

She came upon a clearing she had never seen before, though she knew every inch of the surrounding land. At its center stood an ancient tree, its massive roots twisting into the earth like veins. The air around it was thick with energy, and Nanny's heart quickened as she approached.

"You've brought me here," she whispered, her voice steady despite the weight of the moment. "What is it you wish to show me?"

A breeze stirred the branches, and the faint scent of her grandmother's herbal remedies filled the air. Nanny closed her eyes, allowing the memories to flood her mind. She saw her grandmother's weathered hands grinding leaves, heard her voice chanting prayers, and felt the warmth of the fire in their home.

"You carry more than the burden of leadership," her grandmother's voice echoed in her mind. "You carry the spirits of those who came before you. They will guide you when the time comes."

That night, Nanny shared her experience with Sekesu as they sat outside their home, Ama asleep inside. "I felt them, Sekesu," she said, her voice filled with awe. "Our ancestors. They were there, in the forest. They're watching, waiting."

Sekesu's eyes widened, but she nodded. "We've always known they're with us. But why now? What do they want?"

Nanny shook her head. "I don't know. But I feel as though they're preparing us for something. Perhaps it's a warning, or perhaps it's a reminder that we are not alone."

Sekesu reached for her sister's hand. "Whatever it is, we'll face it together. Just as we always have."

The whispers grew stronger in the following days. During a meeting with the village elders, Nanny felt an urge to speak of her experience. The elders listened intently, their expressions thoughtful.

"The spirits do not speak without purpose," Elder Kwame said, his voice low and reverent. "They may be urging us to prepare. Peace does not last forever, and we must not grow complacent."

Nanny nodded. "We will fortify our defenses and ensure everyone is ready. But we will also honor the spirits. They have guided us this far, and they deserve our gratitude."

The council agreed, and plans were made for a ceremony to honor the ancestors. The village would gather under the great silk cotton tree, their voices rising in song and prayer, their offerings a token of their respect.

On the night of the ceremony, the air was thick with anticipation. The villagers gathered, their faces illuminated by the flickering light of torches. Nanny stood at the center, her spear planted firmly in the ground beside her. Adisa was by her side, his presence a steadying force.

As the chants began, the forest seemed to come alive. The rustling leaves joined the rhythm, and the air shimmered with a quiet power. Nanny closed her eyes, her heart swelling with a sense of connection that transcended time and place.

"We honor you," she whispered, her voice carried by the wind. "Guide us, protect us, and give us the strength to face what lies ahead."

The ceremony ended with a sense of renewed purpose. The Maroons returned to their homes, their spirits lifted, their unity reaffirmed. But Nanny knew this was only the beginning. The ancestors had spoken, and she would not ignore their call. The peace they cherished was precious, but it was fragile. And Nanny was ready to defend it—with the strength of her people and the wisdom of those who had come before.

Chapter 25
Shadows in the Night

The night was calm, the kind of serene quiet that only the Blue Mountains could provide. Nanny tucked Ama into her small bed, the child's soft breathing already settling into the rhythm of sleep. A gentle smile crossed Nanny's face as she placed a kiss on her daughter's forehead. Her other hand rested lightly on her rounded belly, the life within stirring slightly as if sensing the peaceful moment.

Outside, the faint glow of firelight flickered through the window. Adisa's voice carried softly into the room, humming a tune that Nanny recognized from their homeland. She stepped into the main room of their hut and paused. Adisa sat at the wooden table, his hands deftly working with ink made from wild berries and charcoal. His focus was intense, his movements purposeful as he carefully painted on a stretched piece of bark.

"What are you doing?" Nanny asked, curiosity piqued.

Adisa glanced up briefly, his lips curving into a secretive smile. "It's not ready yet."

Nanny stepped closer, trying to catch a glimpse of his work, but Adisa slid his arm over the painting, shielding it. "You'll see when it's finished," he said, his tone playful.

"You're hiding something," Nanny teased, folding her arms. "And you know I don't like secrets."

Adisa chuckled, his eyes twinkling. "This one, you'll forgive me for."

Before Nanny could press further, a sharp knock sounded at the door. The tone was urgent, cutting through the quiet like a blade. Both Nanny and Adisa froze for a moment before exchanging a glance. Adisa rose, his hand instinctively brushing the hilt of his blade as he moved to open the door.

Standing in the doorway was Kojo, one of the village scouts. His face was drawn, his breathing heavy as though he had run the entire way.

"Nanny," Kojo said, his voice low but firm. "They've returned. The British."

Nanny's heart clenched, but her expression remained calm. "How many?"

"Dozens," Kojo replied. "Perhaps more. They've set up camp not far from the western ridge. Their numbers are greater than before, and they're carrying supplies. It looks like they mean to stay."

Adisa cursed under his breath, his hand tightening into a fist. Nanny's mind raced, calculating the next steps even as her body remained still.

"How close did you get?" she asked.

"Close enough to see their movement patterns," Kojo said. "They're scouting the area, but they haven't found our defenses yet. We still have the element of surprise."

Nanny nodded. "Good work, Kojo. Gather the other scouts and bring them to the council meeting place. We'll need every detail you can provide."

Kojo bowed slightly and disappeared into the night. Nanny turned to Adisa, who was already strapping on his weapons. "This is what we've prepared for," he said, his voice steady but tinged with anger. "They won't catch us off guard."

Nanny moved to him, placing a hand on his arm. "We will face them," she said. "But we must be smart. The people are depending on us, not just to fight, but to protect what we've built here."

Adisa met her gaze, his resolve mirrored in her eyes. "I trust your lead, Nanny. Always."

She nodded, drawing strength from his presence. Then, turning back toward the room where Ama slept, she whispered a silent promise.

"For them," she said to herself, her hand briefly brushing the growing life within her. "For all of us."

Within the hour, the village council gathered under the great silk cotton tree. Torches lit the clearing, casting long shadows as the leaders exchanged information and devised their strategy. The atmosphere was tense but determined. Nanny stood at the center, her voice steady as she outlined the plan.

"We will not let them take this land," she said, her tone firm. "But we must act swiftly. Their supplies mean they plan to settle in, and we cannot allow that. We strike before dawn, when their guard is weakest."

The warriors nodded, their faces set with grim determination. Adisa stepped forward, his voice carrying over the murmurs. "We will fight as one, just as we always have. For our families, for our freedom."

The crowd responded with a unified cheer, their spirits bolstered by the strength of their leaders. As the meeting ended and the warriors dispersed to prepare, Nanny stood beneath the ancient tree, her spear in hand. The whispers of her ancestors seemed to surround her, their presence a steadying force.

"We are ready," she whispered to the night. "And we will prevail."

Chapter 26
A Fractured Peace

The first light of dawn crept through the thick foliage of the Blue Mountains as Nanny walked back to her hut, her thoughts heavy with the preparations for the looming battle. She barely had a moment to rest when a shout from the village perimeter drew her attention. A group of scouts had returned, escorting several newly escaped slaves and refugees from nearby villages.

The newcomers were gaunt and weary, their clothes tattered, and their faces bore the marks of hardship. Despite their condition, their eyes burned with a mixture of hope and fear. Nanny immediately made her way to the gathering, Adisa close behind her.

One of the scouts stepped forward. "Nanny, these are our brothers and sisters from the lowlands. They've escaped the British and brought news."

The tallest of the refugees, a man with deep scars on his arms, stepped forward. "The British," he began, his voice hoarse. "They're more ruthless now than ever. They burn everything in their path. Villages, farms, even the forests… nothing is spared."

Another woman, cradling a young child, added, "They're poisoning the streams too. We saw them pouring something into the water. People fell ill within hours, some didn't survive."

A murmur of shock rippled through the gathered Maroons. Adisa's jaw tightened, his hand resting on the hilt of his blade. Nanny raised her hand, quieting the group.

"You are safe now," she assured the refugees. "You will rest here, and we will ensure you have food and water. But we must hear all you know about the British movements."

After ensuring the newcomers were settled, Nanny returned to her hut to prepare for the council meeting. As she entered, she accidentally bumped into the table where Adisa had been working the previous night. A rolled piece of bark fell to the floor, partially unfurling. Curious, Nanny bent to pick it up, her eyes widening as she took in the image.

It was a painting of her. Adisa had captured her every essence with such precision and detail that it almost seemed alive. Her strength and grace radiated from the ink and charcoal, her eyes fierce and steady. The berries had lent a vibrancy to the piece, and the delicate lines of her braided hair and the intricate patterns on her gown seemed to dance on the bark.

For a moment, Nanny forgot everything else, her fingers brushing the edges of the artwork. She smiled, a rare and tender expression. "Adisa," she murmured, her voice filled with quiet awe. "Why didn't you show me this?"

Adisa entered the room, stopping when he saw her holding the painting. His face softened into a sheepish smile. "I wanted it to be a surprise," he said. "You're always so busy leading. I thought you might like something just for you."

"It's beautiful," Nanny said, her voice thick with emotion. "Thank you."

But as her eyes lingered on the painting, a strange thought crossed her mind. The precision of the details reminded her of something else—the map she had burned in the British command tent. Shaking off the memory, she rolled the painting carefully and set it aside. There was more pressing business at hand.

The council meeting began under the silk cotton tree, where the scouts and refugees shared their harrowing accounts in detail.

"They've fortified their camp at the western ridge," one scout reported. "But their patrols are sloppy. They rely too much on their numbers and their weapons."

"Their poison will be their greatest weapon," another added. "We must secure our water sources and warn the other villages."

Nanny listened intently, her mind already crafting a plan. "We will send scouts to monitor their camp closely," she said. "Our warriors will prepare for a strike, but only when we have the advantage. In the meantime, we must protect our streams and ensure the safety of our people."

Elder Kwame stepped forward, his voice grave. "This poison is a new kind of evil. It shows they are not just trying to defeat us; they mean to destroy everything. We must be ready for anything."

The council nodded in agreement, their determination unshaken despite the grim news.

As the meeting adjourned, Nanny lingered beneath the tree, her thoughts heavy. Adisa joined her, his hand resting lightly on her shoulder.

"We will face this," he said, his voice steady. "And we will overcome it. Together."

Nanny turned to him, her expression resolute. "Yes. For our children, for our people, and for the future we're building."

The forest around them seemed to echo her words, the rustling leaves whispering their quiet support. The Maroons had faced impossible odds before, and they would again. Nanny's heart swelled with both love and resolve as she prepared for the battles yet to come.

Chapter 27

The Gathering Storm

The quiet hum of daily life in Moore Town was now laced with tension. The news of the British's ruthless tactics had unsettled even the most steadfast Maroons. Yet, amidst the unease, preparations moved forward. Scouts left at dawn to monitor the enemy's camp, warriors sharpened their weapons, and the village elders strategized under the great silk cotton tree. Nanny, as always, was at the center of it all, her presence a beacon of strength.

Early in the day, another group of refugees arrived, their appearance as haggard as those before them. Among them was a young boy, no more than ten, clutching a bundle wrapped in cloth. Nanny knelt to his level, her voice gentle.

"What is your name?"

"Kwesi," the boy said, his voice barely above a whisper.

"You are safe now, Kwesi," Nanny assured him. "What is in your bundle?"

The boy hesitated, then slowly unwrapped the cloth to reveal a small calabash filled with murky water. "It's from our village stream," he said. "The soldiers poured something into it. My father said to bring it to someone who could help."

Nanny took the calabash carefully, her expression darkening. "You've done well, Kwesi. Rest now, and we will take care of this."

She handed the calabash to Sekesu, who had been standing nearby. "Take this to the healers," Nanny instructed. "We need to know what's in this water."

Sekesu nodded, her face grim, and hurried away.

Later that evening, Nanny found herself back at her hut. The weight of leadership pressed heavily on her, but the sight of Adisa with Ama in his lap brought her a brief moment of peace. He was telling their daughter a story, his voice animated as he recounted the tale of Anansi and the Sky God. Ama's laughter filled the room, a sound so pure it momentarily chased away Nanny's worries.

"You're home early," Adisa said, looking up as Nanny entered.

"Not early enough," she replied, smiling faintly. "It's good to see her laugh."

Adisa set Ama down and rose to his feet, crossing the room to Nanny. "And it's good to see you take a moment to breathe."

She sighed, leaning into him. "There's so much to do. The poison in the streams, the British… it feels endless."

"That's why we're here," Adisa said, his voice steady. "To share the weight. You're not alone in this."

Before Nanny could reply, a sharp knock came at the door. Adisa opened it to reveal Elder Kwame, his expression grave.

"Nanny, we have news," he said. "The scouts have returned. They've found the British's main camp. It's larger than we anticipated, and they've fortified it well. They're also amassing more soldiers."

Nanny's jaw tightened. "We'll call a council meeting immediately. Let the scouts rest for now, but I want a full report from them before the night is over."

Kwame nodded and departed as quickly as he'd arrived. Nanny turned back to Adisa, her eyes reflecting both determination and concern.

"It's starting," she said. "We need to be ready."

"We will be," Adisa assured her. "But don't forget, Nanny, this village stands because of you. Trust in what you've built."

The council gathered under the silk cotton tree as the moon rose high above. The scouts detailed the British camp's layout, describing rows of tents, stockpiles of weapons, and guards patrolling the perimeter.

"They've poisoned every stream near their camp," one scout reported. "They mean to force us out by destroying the land itself."

Nanny listened intently, her mind already piecing together a strategy. "If they want us to abandon this land, they will be sorely disappointed," she said. "We'll move swiftly and strike decisively. But first, we need to ensure our people's safety. Fortify the village, protect our water sources, and prepare for battle."

Elder Kwame spoke up. "And what of the poison in the streams? Even if we defeat them, the land will bear their scars."

Nanny nodded, her expression grim. "I'll consult the healers and the elders. There must be a way to cleanse the water. We will not let this land die."

The meeting ended with a renewed sense of purpose. As the Maroons dispersed to carry out their tasks, Nanny remained beneath the silk cotton tree, staring into the distance. The forest around her seemed to hum with quiet energy, its ancient presence a reminder of the resilience she drew upon.

"We'll endure," she whispered to the night. "Just as we always have."

Chapter 28
A Change in the Tides

The morning after the council meeting, Moore Town was alive with activity. Warriors gathered in groups, refining their tactics, while women and elders fortified the village. Yet, an undercurrent of unease rippled through the community. The poisoned streams weighed heavily on everyone's minds.

Nanny stood outside the healer's hut, her expression grave. Inside, Sekesu and the elders had been examining the water sample Kwesi had brought. When Sekesu emerged, the look on her face told Nanny everything she needed to know.

"There's nothing we can do," Sekesu said quietly. "The poison is too potent. Even with all our remedies, the water is beyond saving."

A wave of silence passed over the small group gathered around. Nanny's fingers tightened around the spear in her hand. "Then we'll have to find another way. What do you suggest?"

Elder Kwame stepped forward, his voice calm but firm. "We must rely on the underground waters and the head of the streams. The British haven't reached those yet. We can dig for fresh springs and use the uppermost sources of the rivers. It will be harder work, but it's our best chance."

Nanny nodded, already calculating the manpower needed for such a task. "Then we'll start immediately. Every family will be assigned shifts to help. We will not let this break us."

Later that day, Nanny sat at the edge of the forest, sharpening her spear. The rhythmic sound of the blade against the stone was grounding, but her mind churned with questions. Could they secure enough water for the entire village? Would the British poison those sources too?

Adisa approached, his steps light but deliberate. He carried an air of calm, though Nanny could see the tension in his jaw.

"The warriors are ready," he said, sitting beside her. "They're waiting for your signal."

Nanny paused, her gaze fixed on the horizon. "And the scouts?"

"They've confirmed the British camp is poorly guarded at night," Adisa replied. "Their supply wagons are exposed, and their sentries are scattered. We have a clear opportunity to strike."

Nanny's lips pressed into a thin line. "Good. But we'll need to act swiftly. The longer we wait, the more damage they'll do to the land."

Adisa placed a hand on her shoulder. "You're carrying a heavy burden. Remember, you don't have to carry it alone."

She glanced at him, her expression softening. "I know. But this land, these people… they're my responsibility. I can't afford to falter."

"And you won't," Adisa said firmly. "We're all with you. Always."

As night fell, the Maroons gathered under the silk cotton tree. The warriors stood ready, their weapons glinting in the torchlight. The elders formed a semicircle, their voices low as they blessed the warriors and the mission ahead.

Nanny stood at the center, her spear in hand, her voice strong as she addressed her people. "The British think they can break us by poisoning our streams and burning our land. But they don't know who we are. We are Maroons, and we do not surrender."

The crowd murmured their agreement, their resolve solidifying. Nanny continued, "We will fight not just for survival, but for the future of our children, for the freedom of those yet to come. We will show them that this land belongs to us."

The cheers that erupted were deafening, the unity of the Maroons tangible in the night air. Nanny raised her spear high. "Let us remind them why the Blue Mountains have never been conquered."

With that, the warriors dispersed into the forest, their movements silent and purposeful. Nanny lingered for a moment, her gaze turning to the heavens. The stars seemed brighter tonight, their light a quiet promise of hope.

"Guide us," she whispered to the ancestors. "And give us strength."

Then, she turned and followed her people into the night, her resolve unshaken. The battle ahead would be fierce, but the Maroons were ready, their spirits unbroken and their unity stronger than ever.

Chapter 29

Into the Trap

The moon hung high above the Blue Mountains, its light casting silver streaks across the dense forest as the Maroons advanced toward the British camp. Led by Adisa, the warriors moved with practiced stealth, their footsteps silent against the forest floor. The scouts had reported that the camp was poorly guarded, its defenses spread thin. It seemed an opportunity too good to ignore.

As they neared the perimeter, the faint glow of British torches came into view. Adisa raised a hand, signaling for the group to halt. He turned back to his warriors, his voice barely above a whisper.

"We strike quickly and retreat before they have time to organize. Aim for their supply wagons and their munitions."

The warriors nodded, their faces resolute. Adisa's gaze lingered on the group, his confidence in their unity unshaken. He motioned for them to advance.

The initial moments of the attack were precise and devastating. Maroon warriors descended upon the camp like shadows, their arrows and spears striking true. The British sentries, caught off guard, scrambled to respond. Flames erupted as a supply wagon was set alight, the fire spreading rapidly to nearby tents. Cries of alarm echoed through the camp as the Maroons pressed their advantage.

But then, the trap was sprung.

From the surrounding darkness, rows of British soldiers emerged, their muskets already aimed. Hidden detachments poured into the camp from every direction, encircling the Maroons. The warriors, realizing too late the extent of the ruse, found themselves overwhelmed.

"Hold the line!" Adisa shouted, his voice cutting through the chaos. He fought fiercely, his blade flashing in the firelight as he struck down soldier after soldier. Around him, the Maroons fought with equal ferocity, their movements honed by years of survival in the mountains. But the British numbers were overwhelming.

The air was thick with smoke and the clash of steel. Maroon warriors fell one by one, their cries of pain fueling the remaining fighters. Adisa's heart pounded as he fought his way toward the munitions store. If he could destroy it, they might still have a chance to escape.

He reached the barrels of powder, but before he could act, a sharp pain shot through his side. Looking down, he saw the glint of a bayonet. A British soldier wrenched the weapon free, and Adisa staggered, blood staining his tunic. He gritted his teeth, summoning the last of his strength to light a torch and throw it toward the barrels.

The explosion rocked the camp, a deafening roar that sent debris flying. The sudden chaos gave the remaining Maroons a fleeting chance to retreat. Adisa collapsed to the ground, his vision blurring as his warriors pulled him away from the flames.

By the time the Maroons regrouped in the forest, their numbers had been decimated. Nanny was waiting for them at a predetermined safe zone, her heart sinking as she saw the wounded and the fallen. When she spotted Adisa being carried by two warriors, her breath caught.

"Adisa!" she cried, rushing to his side. She knelt beside him, her hands trembling as she pressed cloth to his wound. His face was pale, but his eyes met hers with a flicker of determination.

"It was a trap," he said weakly. "They knew we would come. They were waiting."

Nanny's jaw tightened, her mind racing. "Rest now," she said, her voice firm but gentle. "We'll get you to the healers. You've done enough."

Around them, the surviving warriors looked to Nanny, their faces etched with grief and exhaustion. She rose, her expression resolute despite the weight of the loss.

"We will not let their sacrifice be in vain," she said, her voice carrying through the clearing. "The British think they can break us, but they will only strengthen our resolve. We will regroup, we will rebuild, and we will fight again. This land is ours, and we will not surrender it."

The warriors nodded, their spirits bolstered by her words. As they moved to tend to the wounded and lay their fallen comrades to rest, Nanny remained by Adisa's side, her hand clutching his.

"You're going to be fine," she whispered, more to herself than to him. "We're going to survive this. Together."

The forest around them seemed to echo her vow, the rustling leaves a reminder of the ancestors who watched over them. The battle had been a devastating blow, but the Maroons' spirit remained unbroken. They would endure, just as they always had.

Chapter 30

The Weight of Silence

When the Maroons returned to Moore Town, the village was plunged into chaos. The usual harmony of daily life had been replaced with frantic activity. Women and elders moved quickly between the wounded, applying herbal poultices and murmuring prayers. Children, sensing the tension, remained quiet and out of the way. Smoke from the cooking fires mingled with the acrid scent of blood and burnt fabric.

Nanny stood in the center of it all, her face a mask of calm despite the turmoil around her. Adisa lay in the healer's hut, his wounds carefully tended but still deep. The sight of him unconscious, his breathing labored, had shaken Nanny more than she cared to admit. Yet, she forced herself to focus on the tasks at hand.

The Maroons had never suffered such heavy casualties before. The warriors who had returned bore not only physical wounds but also the weight of losing so many of their comrades. Their eyes were haunted, their movements slower than before. It was a blow to their morale, and Nanny knew it.

"We cannot falter," she told Sekesu as they worked side by side, preparing salves. "If the British advance, we need every hand ready."

Sekesu nodded grimly. "But they haven't moved yet. It's been days, and there's no sign of them leaving their camp. What are they waiting for?"

Nanny's brow furrowed. That same question had gnawed at her since their return. The British had every advantage now—their numbers, their resources, even the element of surprise. And yet, they remained stagnant, as if waiting for some unseen signal.

The following night, Nanny called a council meeting under the great silk cotton tree. The elders and the remaining warriors gathered, their faces lit by the soft glow of torches. The mood was somber, the weight of their recent losses heavy in the air.

"The British have not advanced," Nanny began, her voice steady but laced with urgency. "We must determine why. Are they regrouping? Waiting for reinforcements? Or is this another trap?"

Elder Kwame stroked his beard thoughtfully. "They may be trying to break our spirits. To make us doubt ourselves."

"Or they could be waiting for a signal from one of their allies," Sekesu added. "If they're planning something larger, we need to act before they do."

A young scout stepped forward. "Their camp has remained quiet," he reported. "But they've reinforced their defenses. More soldiers are patrolling the perimeter, and they've set up barriers around their supplies."

Nanny's eyes narrowed. "They're expecting us to attack again. They want us to come to them on their terms."

The council murmured in agreement. One of the warriors, his arm in a sling, spoke up. "If we wait too long, they'll gain more ground. But if we rush in again, we risk another ambush."

Nanny nodded. "We need a plan that forces them out of their camp. Something that puts them on the defensive, where they can't rely on their numbers or their traps."

Elder Kwame's eyes gleamed with an idea. "If we cut off their access to resources, they'll have no choice but to move. Their water, their food… if we make these scarce, they'll come to us."

"It's risky," Sekesu said. "But it might work. We know this land better than they ever could. We can use that to our advantage."

Nanny glanced around the circle, reading the determination on every face. "Then it's decided. We'll strike at their lifelines. Scouts will map out their supply routes, and warriors will prepare to intercept them. The British think they have the upper hand, but we'll remind them why the Blue Mountains have never fallen."

The council dispersed, the mood shifting from despair to resolve. The plan was dangerous, but it was their best chance to regain the upper hand.

That night, Nanny sat alone outside the healer's hut, her spear resting beside her. The stars above seemed brighter than usual, their light a quiet comfort. From inside, she could hear Adisa's faint breathing. It was steady now, a sign that he was healing. But the memory of him collapsing in the British camp still haunted her.

"We'll endure," she whispered to herself. "For you, for our children, for our people."

The forest around her seemed to hum with agreement, the whispers of her ancestors mingling with the rustling leaves. The battle was far from over, but Nanny's resolve burned brighter than ever. The British might be waiting, but so were the Maroons. And when the time came, they would strike with the strength of the mountains behind them.

Chapter 31

Smoke and Strategy

The morning air was cool, a deceptive calm that belied the tension gripping Moore Town. Nanny led a small group of scouts and warriors through the forest, their mission clear: locate and disrupt the British supply lines. The group moved with precision, their steps silent against the soft earth. Nanny, though visibly pregnant, was as swift and agile as ever, her spear in hand and her senses heightened.

As they advanced deeper into the forest, something caught Nanny's attention. She halted abruptly, her keen eyes scanning the surroundings. Then it hit her—a distinct, acrid scent carried by the wind. Smoke.

"Do you smell that?" she asked, her voice low but urgent.

The warriors paused, sniffing the air. One of them nodded. "It's smoke. Close."

Nanny's heart quickened. Without hesitation, she darted toward a nearby ridge, her movements swift despite her condition. From the high vantage point, the full extent of the situation came into view. Below, the forest was ablaze, flames consuming everything in their path. Thick columns of smoke billowed upward, carried by the wind toward the Blue Mountains.

Her stomach churned as she realized the scope of the British plan. They weren't simply cutting off resources—they were waging war against the land itself. The fire wasn't just destruction; it was a weapon, and the wind was their ally.

The warriors who had followed her to the ridge gasped at the sight. One of them, a young man named Kojo, spoke with disbelief. "They're burning everything. The forest, the streams... everything."

Nanny's jaw tightened. "It's not just destruction," she said, her voice steady but cold. "The wind will carry the smoke up the mountains, choking us out. They're trying to force us to surrender without ever setting foot in our village."

Kojo looked at her, his face pale. "What do we do?"

Nanny's mind raced. The fire was vast, too much for their small group to combat directly. Returning to the village would take time they couldn't afford. She clenched her fists, anger bubbling beneath her calm exterior. Despite the brutality of the act, she couldn't help but admire the cunning of the British general. It was a calculated move, ruthless but brilliant.

"We go back to Moore Town," she said finally. "We need to prepare for the smoke. Water, cloths, anything that can shield us. And we send a message to the other villages. They need to know what's coming."

The journey back to Moore Town was fraught with tension. Nanny's mind replayed the scene of the burning forest, each detail fueling her resolve. By the time they reached the village, the first wisps of smoke had begun to creep over the ridges.

The villagers sprang into action as Nanny relayed the news. Buckets of water were placed around the village, and damp cloths were distributed to cover mouths and noses. The elders worked quickly to gather herbs that could help with the effects of smoke inhalation, their knowledge of the land once again proving invaluable.

Sekesu approached Nanny as she coordinated the efforts. "Do you think they'll come after the smoke reaches us?"

Nanny shook her head. "No. They don't need to. If the smoke does its job, they'll expect us to flee the mountains. They're trying to break us without another battle."

"But they underestimate us," Sekesu said, her voice firm.

Nanny nodded, a flicker of a smile breaking through her grim expression. "They always do."

As night fell, the smoke grew thicker, its acrid sting seeping into the village. Families huddled together, damp cloths pressed to their faces. Despite the discomfort, the villagers remained resolute, their trust in Nanny unwavering.

At the edge of the village, Nanny stood with Adisa, who had insisted on joining her despite his injuries. His face was pale, but his eyes burned with determination.

"They think they can choke us out," he said, his voice rasping. "But they don't know who they're dealing with."

Nanny placed a hand on his arm. "Rest, Adisa. You've done enough."

"Not while you're still fighting," he replied, his tone leaving no room for argument.

Nanny turned her gaze to the horizon, where the glow of the fire still lit the sky. The smoke curled upward like a living thing, its tendrils reaching ever closer. She took a deep breath, her resolve solidifying.

"We'll endure," she said quietly. "And when this is over, we'll remind them why the Blue Mountains belong to us."

The forest around them seemed to hum in agreement, the ancient spirits lending their strength. The Maroons had faced impossible odds before, and they would again. The British had brought the fire, but they had yet to see the storm that Nanny and her people would unleash in return.

Chapter 32

Cracks in the Mountain

The acrid smoke enveloped Moore Town, transforming the once-thriving village into a shadow of itself. The air was so thick that even the strongest warriors struggled to see their hands in front of their faces. Children coughed violently, their small bodies wracked with illness. Elders and the wounded, already vulnerable, succumbed quickly to the poisonous haze. The cries of grief and pain echoed through the village, a sound that pierced Nanny's soul.

Every breath was a battle. The villagers tried to shield themselves with damp cloths, but it wasn't enough. The smoke seeped into every crevice, a constant reminder of the British's brutal strategy. Maroons from other villages arrived in small groups, seeking refuge from the spreading fire. Their presence strained the already scarce resources, and the once-unshakeable unity of Moore Town began to falter.

Plans to descend the mountain were whispered among the villagers. For the first time, the idea of leaving their sacred home felt like a real possibility. But Nanny stood firm, her resolve unwavering even as tears streaked her soot-stained face. She had never felt so close to breaking.

That evening, Nanny found herself pacing outside her hut, her mind racing. She had barely slept in days, her thoughts consumed by the growing crisis. As she turned, her gaze fell on Adisa. He was sitting near the fire, sharpening his blade, his movements slow but deliberate. The sight of him stirred something deep within her—a mix of anger and suspicion that she could no longer suppress.

She stormed toward him, her spear gripped tightly in her hand.

"Adisa," she said, her voice sharp. "I need to ask you something."

He looked up, his brow furrowing at her tone. "What is it?"

"The map," she began, her words clipped. "The one I found in the British camp. It was drawn on goatskin, with markings of our village. It was detailed, too detailed to be random. I want to know why it looked exactly like your drawings."

Adisa's face paled. "Nanny, I don't know what you're talking about."

"Don't lie to me!" she snapped, her spear pointing at his chest. "Was it yours? Did you give it to someone? Or did you leave it behind for them to find?"

Adisa stood slowly, raising his hands in a gesture of peace. "I would never betray you, Nanny. You know that. Yes, it's possible it was mine. I draw all the time, you know that. I give them away to children, to villagers. It's how I relax. But I would never…"

"Relax?" she interrupted, her voice trembling with fury. "Your 'relaxation' may have cost us everything! That map—it's how they knew where to strike, how to trap us."

Adisa stepped closer, his voice pleading. "If it was mine, it was unintentional. You have to believe me. I've fought beside you, bled beside you. I would never betray my people or you."

But Nanny wasn't ready to relent. Her spear was at his throat now, her eyes blazing with a mix of rage and despair. The villagers who had gathered around the confrontation watched in stunned silence, their trust in their leaders hanging by a thread.

"If you've betrayed us," Nanny said, her voice low and dangerous, "I will not hesitate to end it here."

Adisa held her gaze, his expression unwavering. "I swear on my life and the lives of our children, I am loyal to you, Nanny. To the Maroons. If you doubt me, then kill me. But know that I have done nothing to harm you or our people."

For a long moment, the world seemed to hold its breath. Then, slowly, Nanny lowered her spear. Tears welled in her eyes as she turned away, her shoulders trembling.

"I want to believe you," she said softly, almost to herself. "But everything is falling apart, and I don't know who to trust anymore."

Adisa stepped forward but stopped himself, giving her the space she needed. "Then let me prove it to you," he said. "Whatever it takes, I'll make this right."

That night, the village remained in a state of uneasy quiet. The smoke grew heavier, its tendrils creeping through the trees like ghostly fingers. The children's coughing echoed through the night, a cruel reminder of their vulnerability. Nanny sat alone by the fire, her spear across her lap. Her mind was a storm of doubts and fears, but beneath it all, a flicker of hope remained.

She knew one thing for certain: the Maroons would endure. They had to. The Blue Mountains were more than their home—they were a symbol of freedom, a testament to their strength. And no matter the cost, Nanny would fight to preserve that legacy.

Chapter 33

Loss Beyond Measure

The oppressive smoke hung thick in the air, smothering the remnants of hope in Moore Town. Nanny walked alongside her sister, Sekesu, their conversation a rare respite from the chaos. They moved slowly, weaving through the coughing children and weary elders, each face a reminder of the devastation that surrounded them.

"I'm breaking, Sekesu," Nanny admitted, her voice barely above a whisper. "Every cough, every tear, every grave we dig… it feels like a piece of me dies with them."

Sekesu reached for her sister's hand, her grip firm and steady. "You're stronger than this, Nanny. You always have been. But you don't have to carry it all alone."

Nanny nodded, though her heart remained heavy. "It's hard to see the way forward when all I see is suffering."

They walked in silence for a moment, the weight of unspoken fears pressing between them. Then, suddenly, Nanny stopped, her hand flying to her abdomen. A sharp, searing pain shot through her body, stealing her breath. She gasped, doubling over.

"Nanny!" Sekesu cried, rushing to her side. "What's wrong?"

"The baby," Nanny managed, her voice strained. "It's too early... something's wrong."

Sekesu wasted no time. She called for help, her voice cutting through the din of the village. Two warriors hurried over, lifting Nanny carefully and carrying her toward the healer's hut. The villagers watched in stunned silence, their leader's pain a visceral reminder of their own fragility.

Inside the healer's hut, the air was thick with the scent of herbs and desperation. Nanny lay on a mat, her body wracked with pain. Sekesu knelt beside her, gripping her hand tightly, while the healer worked with frantic precision, murmuring prayers under her breath.

Nanny's breaths came in short, ragged gasps. Sweat beaded her forehead, her normally fierce eyes clouded with pain and fear. She gritted her teeth, refusing to cry out, but the agony was overwhelming.

"You need to push," the healer urged. "The baby is coming."

"It's too soon," Sekesu whispered, tears streaming down her face.

Nanny clenched her jaw, her body trembling as she followed the healer's instructions. Each push felt like it tore her apart, the pain blinding. Time seemed to stretch endlessly, the muffled sounds of the village fading into the background.

Finally, after what felt like an eternity, the room fell silent. The healer cradled the tiny, motionless form in her hands, her face etched with sorrow. Nanny's head fell back against the mat, her chest heaving as she fought to catch her breath.

"Why can't I hear him?" Nanny asked weakly, her voice trembling.

The healer didn't answer immediately. Instead, she wrapped the baby in a soft cloth and placed him gently in Nanny's arms.

"He... he didn't survive," the healer said, her voice breaking.

Nanny stared at the tiny face, so perfect yet so still. Her heart shattered, the weight of the loss crashing over her like a tidal wave. Tears streamed down her cheeks as she clutched the lifeless form to her chest, a raw, guttural sob escaping her lips.

Sekesu wrapped her arms around her sister, her own tears falling freely. "I'm so sorry, Nanny. I'm so sorry."

The room was filled with the sound of grief, a palpable ache that seemed to echo through the walls. Outside, the villagers stood in hushed silence, their hearts heavy with the knowledge that even their unshakable leader was not immune to the cruelty of their circumstances.

Hours later, as the sky darkened, Nanny sat alone in the healer's hut, the baby's small body wrapped in a white cloth beside her. The tears had stopped, but the emptiness remained. She stared at the flickering candlelight, her mind replaying every moment of the past weeks.

Adisa entered quietly, his face lined with sorrow. He knelt beside her, his hand resting gently on her shoulder. "I heard," he said softly. "I… I'm so sorry, Nanny."

She didn't respond immediately. When she finally spoke, her voice was hollow. "I've lost so much, Adisa. Too much. How do I lead when I feel like I've lost everything?"

Adisa took her hand in his, his grip steady. "Because you're Nanny. You are the strength of this village, of our people. And even in your pain, you give us hope. We need you now more than ever."

Nanny turned to him, her eyes filled with tears. "I don't know if I can do this."

"You can," he said firmly. "And you will. Because that's who you are."

She looked down at the small bundle beside her, her heart aching with a grief that would never fully heal. But somewhere deep within, a spark of resolve began to flicker. She would endure. She had to. For her people, for her family, for the memory of the child she had lost.

The fight was far from over, and Nanny knew the path ahead would be harder than ever. But as she rose from the mat, she made a silent vow: she would carry on. For the Maroons, for their freedom, and for the future they had yet to claim.

Chapter 34

A Mother's Grief, A Warrior's Resolve

As dawn broke over the Blue Mountains, Nanny prepared herself for a journey she refused to share with anyone else. The lifeless form of her son, wrapped delicately in white cloth, rested in her arms. Adisa had offered to accompany her, but she had declined, her voice firm though her heart was heavy.

"This is something I must do alone," she said, and there was no arguing with her.

The villagers watched in respectful silence as Nanny disappeared into the forest, her figure soon swallowed by the thick mist. The stillness of the early morning was broken only by the faint rustling of leaves and the occasional call of a bird, a stark contrast to the chaos that had engulfed Moore Town.

Nanny walked deep into the forest, her steps sure but heavy. Each breath she took felt like a battle, the weight of her sorrow pressing down on her chest. She finally stopped at a clearing surrounded by ancient trees, their towering forms a silent testament to the endurance of nature.

She knelt on the earth, her hands trembling as she dug a small grave. The soil was soft, damp from the morning dew, and the task was both cathartic and excruciating. When the grave was ready, she gently placed her son within, his tiny form almost swallowed by the white cloth. Tears blurred her vision as she covered him with earth, each handful feeling like a piece of her own soul being buried.

When the grave was filled, Nanny sat beside it, her body wracked with silent sobs. She cried until there were no more tears, her throat too raw for sound. She cried for her son, for the villagers, for the lives lost in their endless struggle for freedom. And, above all, she cried for her mother and father, for the family she had lost so long ago.

"I need you," she whispered hoarsely. "More than ever. Why did you leave me?"

Exhausted, Nanny leaned against the base of a tree and closed her eyes. Sleep claimed her before she realized it, pulling her into a world that felt both real and surreal.

In the dream—if it was a dream—Nanny was no longer alone. Her mother stood before her, radiant and strong, cradling the stillborn child in her arms. Beside her was Nanny's father, his warrior's stance as proud and commanding as she remembered. Her grandmother was there too, her wise eyes glinting with a mixture of sadness and pride.

"You are not alone, my child," her mother said, her voice like a soothing melody. "We have always been with you, watching over you."

Nanny's breath hitched as she reached out, her fingers brushing her mother's arm. "But I feel so lost," she said, her voice trembling. "Everything is falling apart. I've failed our people, our family."

Her father stepped forward, his deep voice cutting through her despair. "You have not failed, Nanny. This is your trial, your test. A leader's strength is not measured in their victories alone, but in their ability to endure, to rise again after every fall."

Her grandmother spoke next, her tone filled with wisdom. "The ancestors walk with you, child. You carry their strength, their courage. This land is yours to protect, but it is also theirs. Trust in them, and trust in yourself."

Nanny's gaze shifted to her mother, who was now holding the baby closer. "Will he be safe with you?" Nanny asked, her voice breaking.

"Always," her mother replied, a gentle smile on her lips. "He is part of the ancestors now. He will guide you, as we all will."

The vision began to fade, the figures of her family dissolving into the mist. But their words lingered, their presence a comforting weight in her heart.

When Nanny woke, the sun was high in the sky, its light filtering through the canopy above. She looked down at the grave, a sense of peace settling over her despite the lingering ache in her chest. Rising to her feet, she placed a hand on the earth, her fingers pressing into the soil as if to anchor herself to the moment.

"I will not fail," she whispered. "For you, for all of us."

As she made her way back to Moore Town, her steps were lighter, her resolve stronger. The trial was far from over, but Nanny knew she carried the strength of generations within her. And with that, she would face whatever came next.

Chapter 35

The Storm Within and Without

When Nanny returned to Moore Town, there was a shift in the air that even the villagers could feel. The sorrow that had weighed her down seemed to have lifted, replaced by a fierce, unyielding resolve. She walked through the village with purpose, her head held high and her steps steady. The people whispered among themselves, sensing that their leader was once again the Nanny they knew: proud, fierce, and unwavering.

As she passed by a young scout, she stopped briefly, her tone firm but calm.

"Find the elders and gather the war council," she ordered. "We meet immediately."

The scout nodded, darting off without question. Nanny continued her path toward the great silk cotton tree, her presence commanding attention. The villagers watched in awe, some murmuring prayers of thanks, while others exchanged hopeful glances. Whatever burden she had carried into the forest, she had left it there.

The council gathered beneath the ancient tree as dusk began to fall. The elders sat in a semicircle, their faces marked with curiosity and concern. The warriors stood nearby, their weapons in hand, ready to act on Nanny's command. When she arrived, the murmurs ceased. All eyes turned to her.

"Tomorrow," Nanny began, her voice steady and resolute, "we attack."

A wave of shock rippled through the group. Elder Kwame was the first to speak.

"Attack?" he echoed, his brows furrowed. "After all we've suffered, are you certain? The British have the advantage. Their numbers, their firepower—"

Nanny raised a hand, silencing him. "I understand your doubts, and I understand your fear. But something is coming. Something beyond us. The land will fight with us. I can feel it."

Her words hung in the air, heavy with conviction. The council exchanged uneasy glances, but none dared to question her judgment. They had learned long ago that Nanny's instincts were rarely wrong.

"Take the sick, the children, and the elderly to the caves," she continued. "Ensure their safety. The rest of us will prepare for battle. The British think they've broken us, but they will soon learn that we are stronger than they could ever imagine."

The council nodded in agreement, though unease lingered in the air. The meeting concluded swiftly, each member departing to carry out Nanny's orders.

As night fell, the forest seemed to come alive. The winds began to shift, rustling the trees with an urgency that felt almost sentient. Nanny stood at the edge of the village, her spear in hand, watching the sky. The air was thick with humidity, and the distant rumble of thunder echoed through the mountains.

Sekesu approached her, concern etched into her features. "Do you really believe the land will fight with us?"

Nanny turned to her sister, her expression unyielding. "I know it will. The ancestors have spoken. The land knows our struggle. It feels our pain. And now, it will rise with us."

As if in agreement, a powerful gust of wind swept through the trees, carrying with it the faint scent of rain and the promise of a storm. Sekesu shivered, not from the cold, but from the overwhelming sense of something larger at play.

"Nanny," she whispered, "what if this storm is as dangerous as the British?"

Nanny placed a hand on her sister's shoulder, her gaze unwavering. "Danger is unavoidable, Sekesu. But so is our victory. Trust in the land. Trust in me."

By dawn, the storm had begun to take shape. Dark clouds rolled across the sky, their edges illuminated by flashes of lightning. The air was charged with energy, every gust of wind carrying the promise of change. The villagers moved with urgency, their preparations fueled by both fear and hope.

Nanny stood at the center of it all, her presence a steadying force. She raised her spear high, her voice cutting through the howling wind.

"This storm is our ally!" she declared. "It will mask our movements, it will confuse our enemies, and it will remind the British that the Blue Mountains belong to us!"

The crowd erupted in a cheer, their spirits lifted by her unwavering confidence. As the first drops of rain began to fall, Nanny's gaze turned to the horizon. The storm was brewing, both within and without, and she was ready to face it head-on.

Chapter 36

Nature's Wrath

As the storm raged on, Nanny and her warriors descended silently from the mountains toward the British outposts. The wind howled through the trees, carrying with it the whispers of the ancestors, and the rain fell in heavy sheets, cloaking their movements. The warriors were swift and precise, their knowledge of the terrain giving them an undeniable advantage.

The first outpost fell with little resistance. The British soldiers, struggling to manage their weapons and supplies in the worsening storm, were no match for the Maroons' skill and ferocity. Nanny's warriors moved like shadows, striking swiftly and disappearing into the chaos. Each outpost they encountered was similarly overwhelmed, the British caught off guard and unable to regroup.

The main British camp loomed ahead, a stark contrast to the surrounding forest. The British had cleared a large area of trees around the camp, creating an open field to prevent surprise attacks. But in their attempt to control the land, they had unwittingly turned it against themselves.

Nanny raised her hand, signaling her warriors to halt. She stood at the edge of the forest, her sharp eyes scanning the open expanse. Her instincts told her to wait, to let the storm work its magic. The land had already begun to shift in response to the storm's fury.

The first sign of the disaster came as a deep, rumbling groan. The ground beneath the cleared area began to tremble, the rain-soaked soil loosening under the relentless downpour. Nanny's warriors watched in awe as a massive landslide erupted, a cascade of mud and debris sweeping down the slope toward the British camp.

The soldiers had no time to react. Tents, supplies, and men were swallowed by the earth, the destruction swift and merciless. The landslide buried some of the British under layers of mud, while others scrambled for higher ground, only to find their escape routes blocked by the rising waters of nearby streams.

As if the earth's wrath wasn't enough, the poisoned streams—now swollen from the storm—flooded the camp. The water surged with terrifying force, carrying away what remained of the soldiers' defenses. Supplies floated aimlessly, and the panicked cries of the British were drowned out by the roar of the storm.

From the edge of the forest, Nanny and her warriors watched in awe. The storm's fury had done what years of resistance had struggled to achieve: it had decimated the British without a single Maroon life lost in the final assault. The forest seemed alive, its forces converging to drive out the invaders.

Nanny raised her spear, her voice cutting through the downpour. "The ancestors have spoken! The land is ours! Let this be a warning to all who dare to defile it!"

Her warriors erupted into cheers, their voices rising in unison with the storm. They stood in the rain, drenched but triumphant, their spirits lifted by the sight of nature's vengeance. The British camp lay in ruins, the once-formidable force reduced to scattered survivors struggling to escape the unrelenting storm.

As the rain began to ease, Nanny turned to her warriors, her face solemn but proud. "Gather what we can from the wreckage," she commanded. "Weapons, supplies—anything that can aid us. And send scouts to ensure the British do not regroup."

The warriors moved quickly, their victory fueling their determination. Nanny remained at the edge of the forest, her gaze fixed on the destroyed camp. The storm had reminded her of the power of the land

and the spirits that guided it. She knew this victory was not hers alone but shared with the ancestors and the unyielding force of nature.

As her warriors worked, Nanny whispered a prayer of thanks to the land, the storm, and the spirits that had fought alongside them. The battle was over, but the war was far from won. Yet, for the first time in weeks, hope burned brightly in her heart.

The Blue Mountains had proven their loyalty, and the Maroons would continue to fight for the freedom they had carved from the earth itself.

Chapter 37
The White Flag

The storm had passed, leaving behind a landscape scarred by nature's fury. But the Maroons' resolve was unshaken, their victory fueling their next move. Nanny and her warriors pressed on, their pursuit of the fleeing British relentless. They moved with precision, striking quickly and efficiently as the British retreated toward what was left of their ships along the coast.

The outposts that remained were easily overtaken, the British soldiers too demoralized and disorganized to mount a proper defense. Nanny's warriors used what remained of the forest to their advantage, their knowledge of the land unmatched. The British, weary and desperate, were no match for the Maroons' skill.

As they approached the main British encampment near the coast, the scene was one of chaos. Soldiers scrambled to load supplies onto their ships, their movements frantic as the Maroons closed in. The Maroons surrounded the camp, their presence a shadow that loomed over the already broken British forces.

Nanny stood at the forefront, her spear in hand, her eyes scanning the battlefield. Her warriors awaited her command, their weapons ready. Adisa stepped forward, his expression hard.

"They're cornered," he said. "We can end this now, wipe them out for good."

Nanny hesitated, her gaze lingering on the bodies of the fallen British soldiers scattered across the field. Their faces, young and pale, haunted her thoughts. She remembered the words of her father, spoken long ago in her homeland: *Strength is knowing when to fight and when to show mercy.*

The British, realizing their hopeless situation, raised a white flag. A young officer stepped forward, his uniform drenched and his hands trembling.

"We surrender," he called out, his voice carrying over the sound of the waves crashing against the shore. "We ask for mercy."

Adisa's grip on his blade tightened, his anger barely contained. "After all they've done? After the streams, the fires, the lives they've taken? They deserve no mercy."

Nanny turned to him, her expression calm but firm. "And what would killing them achieve? More bloodshed, more hatred? We have already won, Adisa. Let the ancestors see that we are just, even in victory."

Adisa stepped back, his jaw clenched. The other warriors, though reluctant, nodded in agreement. They had trusted Nanny's judgment through countless battles, and they would trust her now.

The Maroons allowed the British to retreat to their ships, but not without a warning. Nanny approached the young officer who had raised the white flag, her presence commanding.

"Tell your leaders," she said, her voice steady and sharp, "that the Blue Mountains are ours. No soldier, no army, will ever take them from us. Return, and you will not leave alive."

The officer nodded, his fear evident. "I will deliver your message."

Nanny stepped back, watching as the British soldiers boarded their ships. The Maroons stood silently, their weapons lowered but their resolve unbroken. The sight of the ships disappearing into the horizon brought a mixture of relief and sadness.

As the rain began to fall again, Nanny turned to her warriors. "Gather the village. The fight is over, but the work is not. We rebuild, and we honor those we've lost."

The warriors nodded, their spirits lifted by her words. The battle had ended, but the story of their resilience would continue. The Blue Mountains, scarred but still standing, were a testament to their strength and unity. And as Nanny stood beneath the darkening sky, she knew her people's freedom had been secured, not just by their hands but by the land and the ancestors who had fought alongside them.

Made in the USA
Columbia, SC
24 May 2025